NEAR DISTANCE

Near Distance

Hanna Stoltenberg

translated by
Wendy H. Gabrielsen

WEATHERGLASS BOOKS

For some years, before she got married and had children, Helene used to smoke. Not a lot, but enough for her to always have a packet of cigarettes in her handbag, and to excuse herself after family dinners and birthday parties to sit on the steps outside, or stand if it was cold, and have a smoke with Karin. When Karin recalls these moments now, they're like aired-out rooms in her mind's eye. She finds herself yearning for them, breathing more deeply and calmly. They had a signal; one would catch the other's eye across the table and hold two fingers discreetly to the mouth. The other adults, and especially Erik, often glanced disapprovingly at mother and daughter as they silently disappeared from the room with their cups of coffee. Karin probably got the blame for passing on this bad habit – after all, she had smoked for years, including when Helene was small – but she didn't care. She enjoyed sharing something with Helene that others disliked and criticized. Karin still remembers the feeling when the front door slammed behind them, shutting out the sound of voices and of plates being scraped clean in the kitchen. Whoever found their lighter first lit the other's cigarette, and then they would inhale and give a sort of sigh together. They didn't usually say much; they made comments about the garden, the neighbours' greenhouse, or they chatted about Helene's student life in Bergen. If Helene asked a question, Karin would sometimes answer honestly about how things were, which she rarely did otherwise. When Helene gave up smoking, she didn't say anything at all. One day she just shook her head when Karin made the sign with her fingers, and after that Karin stopped asking.

It's Sunday morning. The room Karin wakes up in is dark, apart from patches of light coming from either side of the venetian blinds. The man she has spent the weekend with is fast asleep beside her. Before they fell asleep, he made a thing out of finding his boxer shorts in the folds of the duvet and putting them on. She is naked herself. It's tempting to go back to sleep, to delay the inevitable let-down, but she knows it's soon time to leave. Still, she doesn't want to get stressed about it, why should she? Whatever happens now, it's not her problem. She lifts herself up onto her elbows and presses her cheek against her shoulder where the skin is cold. The reading lamp buzzes like an insect when she puts it on, and she turns down the dimmer to make it go quiet. It feels like she has woken up after a general anaesthetic. On a low chest of drawers in front of her, under a massive flat screen, there are two hydrangeas in glazed pots. She picks up her phone from the floor and wipes the lens with a corner of the duvet, then turns the camera towards herself. All her bone structure has disappeared overnight, it seems. She licks her index finger and rubs it under her eyes, blinking against her knuckle to separate her mascara-coated eyelashes. On the bedside table there's a wine glass with a bit of red left at the bottom, some water and Elizabeth Arden hand cream. A pair of reading glasses are folded together on top of a book, which according to a sticker has sold more than one million copies. She studies these things, enjoying the fact that none of them belong to her. She thinks about what he called her the night before. 'Oh baby,' he whispered. 'Baby, baby, baby.'

She's fifty-three.

—

He called himself Mainsail55 and she met him online. After a few messages back and forth, they arranged to meet up for drinks in the city centre. *To get to know each other better*, she wrote, and he answered: *I feel like I know you already.*

As he came towards her his smile was so big that she could make out the silver fillings in his molars. He was wearing a smart grey suit and said he had come straight from the office. At the beginning he gave off a nervous energy that was almost disconcerting, but when they sat down he looked her in the eye without any awkwardness.

After a quick glance at the wine list he ordered a bottle of white, which was placed in an ice bucket on the table. 'I'm glad you agreed to see me,' he said. 'It's not easy meeting new people at our age.'

He looked about sixty himself, maybe a little older. When she smiled, he leaned forward in his chair, with his stomach protruding like a sandbag over his belt.

'Your smile is even lovelier than in your picture,' he said.

'Have you met many women like this?' she asked. 'On the internet?'

'A couple,' he said. 'But it didn't lead to anything. I suppose they weren't great matches, truth be told.' He lay a large hand on top of hers. The hairs on his knuckles caught the light from the lamp hanging low over the table. 'I've never had such a good feeling as I've had today.'

It was her idea to meet there, in that old-fashioned hotel bar, but then he surprised her by inviting her back to his place. Or rather: by wanting to take her there, to show her what it was like. He had moved to Tjuvholmen from Skøyen two years ago, he told her, after the neighbours sold their garden to a property developer who put up a load of 'hideous' functionalist-style houses.

'You don't want to know how much those prefabs went for,' he said, indicating to the waiter that they wanted the bill. 'And then they started jamming trampolines in between the bloody monstrosities – well, that's when I decided I'd had enough.'

She noticed he said *I*, not *we*, but when they got to the flat it was clear he didn't live there alone. There were high boots standing on the shoe racks, and on the chest of drawers lay a sparkling hair clip. She followed him from the hall into the sitting room, which was big and sparsely furnished with a glass table, satin cushions and oval mirrors. An abstract oil painting in bold colours hung over one of the sofas, and two china dogs with long ears looked out across the fjord from the windowsill. From the sitting room they went into the kitchen, a dark room with black varnished cupboard doors and marble worktops. She couldn't believe that the people who lived with these furnishings had left their last home on aesthetic grounds.

'Would you like something?' he asked. 'Wine? Cognac?'

'Wine,' she said. 'Please.'

They took their glasses into the bedroom, then he excused himself and disappeared into the ensuite bathroom. She could hear the hard jet of urine against the toilet bowl as she opened the wardrobe doors. Dresses and long-sleeved silk blouses hung on identical hangers. It didn't bother her that he was married, but by not saying anything he forced her to either pretend or make a scene. In both scenarios she was given a role she didn't like. When he came out of the bathroom, she pulled herself together and let him undress her. She started laughing.

'What are you sniggering at?' he mumbled.

'You. Me. Aren't we ridiculous?'

He stopped abruptly, let go of her left breast and looked at her. 'What do you mean?'

She considered him for a moment, smiled and shook her head.

'Nothing. Forget it.'

She gets out of bed and walks across the room to close the window. Snow-filled clouds hang heavily over Hovedøya, with sunlight stirred in like a spoonful of honey. For a while she stands there looking out, the air cooling the skin on her chest. They had stayed in the whole of the day before, mixed drinks in fluffy dressing gowns and watched films without discussing them afterwards. They ate pizza on the sofa, and reached for each other with greasy fingers. Later on, he lay exhausted on his back and talked about himself, about his niece who was killed by a drunk driver, and the fact that he personally had driven over the limit many times, both before and after. His psychologist had helped him to understand that it had something to do with the feeling of control: he repeated mistakes from the past to prove he could handle their outcome. He didn't know why he was telling her these things, he said, but it felt good to do so. He didn't expect any openness in return.

She forces down the window hook, glancing over her shoulder to make sure he's still asleep. When she was younger, she liked to get out of bed naked almost immediately after having sex with a new man; she would move around in the room freely, lift up objects, leaf through books, make tea. She would return to topics they had discussed earlier in the evening with better, stronger points, as though the act itself was merely a break in an argumentation she was still working on. She wanted to come across as unconquered, and recharge her body with new energy. Later, she had tried to recreate the effect rolled up in a duvet, or a blanket, but the frivolity was gone.

It's nearly eleven o'clock when he wakes up. She's sitting in bed with the book from the bedside table on her lap, a historical novel set in Tudor times.

He reaches over for her earring, holds the stone between his index finger and thumb and twiddles it round in the hole. 'Diamonds?' he says. 'Diamonds mean "invincible", did you know that?'

'They're not real,' she says.

He reaches for his phone, squints sternly at the screen and starts writing something. She realizes she should have left while he was sleeping. He has lots to do, he says apologetically. 'But we can see each other again, can't we, when it's convenient? Convenient for both of us, I mean.'

She spends a long time in the bathroom putting on a new layer of make-up over what's left of the old one. The tiles are green and warm under her feet, and she looks through the cupboards for expensive products to moisturize herself with. Her handbag vibrates on the toilet lid. She washes her hands and dries them on the towel hanging from a silver ring on the wall. She pulls out her phone and straight away her heart beats faster. It's a message from Helene. They haven't seen each other for a couple of months, not since the evening when Karin went over while Endre and the children were in the mountains.

Helene had ordered a takeaway, but gave the impression that it was a luxury she seldom enjoyed, and they chatted about the summer holidays, about the house Helene and Endre had rented with friends in the north of Italy, where it was 'crawling' with Germans. Helene had kept touching the red, flaky skin around her nose, and she looked tired, Karin remembers. It was as if she was talking on autopilot. Karin swipes past the message without reading it – whatever it's about she can't deal with it now, in this bathroom – but it's too late. She pictures Helene in the kitchen, her fingers pressing a jewel-toned capsule into the compartment in the coffee machine, her hand wiping the worktop, shiny rings against the cloth. Her movements are calm and precise. It's a characteristic she has developed as an adult; as a child she was short-tempered and sloppy, impatient if anyone tried to teach her anything. Karin promises herself to answer later, something warm and responsive. Maybe suggest lunch, just the two of them. She knows she's bad at taking the initiative. Her clothes have slipped down into the bath and her sweater has blonde hairs on it that she doubts are hers. She shakes them off briskly and gets dressed.

When she comes into the kitchen he gets off the bar stool. There are several newspapers spread out over the kitchen island. There's a shiny metal bowl filled with avocados and lemons next to an espresso pot and a coffee cup that looks clean.

'Look who it is,' he says with a brief smile. His skin has a damp sheen to it that makes him look younger. A pair of white earbuds lie next to his phone, as if he has been talking to someone.

'Coffee?' she says, nodding at the cup.

He places the back of his hand against the bottom of the pot to see if it's still hot, pours her some coffee and passes it to her. 'I've already finished mine,' he says. 'I can't handle more than one cup in the morning.'

He goes over to the sink, unscrews the espresso pot, rinses each part thoroughly under the tap and knocks the filter hard against the side of the bin. He does all this with his back to her. Afterwards he stands awkwardly, leaning against the worktop with his arms folded. His blue shirt disappears down into dark jeans worn with a narrow, shiny belt. She sits down on one of the high bar stools on the edge of the kitchen island.

'What do you do again?' he says. It sounds harsh, and he

apologizes. 'I know you told me on Friday, but we've had quite a few drinks since then.'

Outside the window snow is leaping in the wind. She feels a rush of sympathy for his poorly concealed desire to get rid of her. If it had been her flat, her spouse, she would have been checking the time too. 'I'm a manager,' she says. 'Of a jewellery shop. Remember? You should drop by one day, if you're in the neighbourhood.'

'I guess you get an employee discount?'

She looks at him, surprised. 'Is there anything you need?'

'No.' He smiles again, shaking his head. 'No, not at all. It's just that – well, you said your earrings weren't real. I just thought that if you worked in a jeweller's—'

'What are you trying to say?'

'What? Nothing. Have I offended you?'

'No.' It goes quiet again. 'I lose them,' she says. 'That's why.'

She unlocks the entrance to her own building with the feeling of having been away a long time. There are damp patches all over the stone floor and a pram parked under the letterboxes. On the way up the stairs she meets one of her neighbours, a young man in a leather jacket and round glasses who lives in the flat below and plays electronic music from his balcony in the summer. Once she saw him with a dark-haired woman in a restaurant, from where she was sitting alone just a few metres away, and she overheard parts of their conversation. He was telling the woman about his family, about his father who was deeply religious, and that he personally had been a member of a Pentecostal church for a short while after he moved to Oslo. Every time Karin sees him now, she pictures him with his palms facing upwards and his eyes closed.

'It's snowing,' she says as she passes him on the landing.

'Is it?' He hesitates, looking first at her, then down at himself.

'I guess I should change my jacket then.'

He arches his back so he can extract his keys from his trouser pocket. She stares at the place where his jacket rides up and reveals a stretch of skin. Then she looks away.

'Thanks for the heads-up!' he says.

She nods, feeling like an old woman.

Inside her front door, she fumbles under the coats to find the light switch. The hall is long and narrow with a kilim rug on the floor and a bathroom at the other end. On the right there's an antique dresser with drawers that can be locked, and on the opposite wall hang two lithographs in simple frames. She puts away her boots on the shoe rack under the coats, carefully zipped up. She has to straighten them a couple of times so they stand properly. If they don't stand right, she can feel it when she's sitting on the sofa or trying to sleep, and then she has to get up and fix it. Her coat is wet from the snow, and she hangs it across two hooks. Out of habit, she goes straight to the mirror over the dresser and looks back at herself as she undoes a few buttons at the neck. She likes looking at herself, always has done. As a child she would often go to the mirror if she felt something strongly, to observe how the different feelings suited her face. She was especially interested in her tears, because they never looked real. Her mother knew what she was up to and would suddenly be standing behind her, telling her to stop looking at herself crying. Still, she never felt ashamed. She simply waited until her mother had gone and resumed her position in front of the mirror.

In the bowl of loose change, she finds a pink hair elastic she can't remember buying and ties her hair into a ponytail. She smoothes back loose hairs before wiping her hands against her skirt. Her knuckles are dry, so she opens the top drawer to look for hand cream. Her phone rings from her bag on the floor. Even before she sees the name on the screen, she knows who it is. She should have answered the message earlier; the friendly tone she had planned to adopt isn't available to her when she's caught off guard. 'Just wait a minute,' she says to Helene. 'Don't hang up.'

She squeezes the phone between her ear and shoulder, finds her cigarettes in her coat pocket and strides briskly into the sitting room. There's a lighter beside the candlestick on the coffee table. She lights a cigarette and smiles fleetingly at the wall to prepare herself.

'Sorry, I'm here now,' she says.

'I sent you a message,' says Helene.

'I know. I was going to answer, but then something came up.'

'Never mind, as long as you got it. Can you make it?'

'Make what?'

'Didn't you read the message?'

'Now I've forgotten what it said.' She sits down on the sofa. Her tights have a ladder by the big toe on one foot, and the varnished nail is sticking though like a false tooth. 'Could you remind me?'

'Can you look after the kids on Saturday? Me and Endre are invited to Ulla and Lars-Erik's. Do you remember them? They were at our wedding. Ulla gave a speech.'

It was a terrible speech. Ulla had cried sharing quite ordinary memories of their friendship as though they expressed something special. Karin had observed Helene to see how she would react, if she had it in her to play this charade for the guests, but she had smiled, apparently moved and sincere. Karin had made a good speech. She cried when she wrote it, but not when she read it out loud.

'This coming Saturday?'

'Yes. Endre's been working so much recently. We could do with a night out with friends.'

'I can't do this Saturday,' says Karin. She's been texting with a man she might meet. They haven't actually set a date or time, but Saturday night seems likely. She scrapes her middle fingernail against the inside of her thumb to stop herself saying any more. 'Sorry,' she says.

'That's okay,' says Helene after a while. 'I'll just call someone else.'

'Is everything all right between you and Endre?'

'What do you mean?'

'You're happy? With him? And with the kids?'

'Yes. Yes, everything's fine. We're great. Why do you always ask that?'

'I just want to be sure you're happy. That's the only thing that matters to me, that you're happy.'

Some clattering noises can be heard in the background, followed by a child screaming. Helene has to go.

Karin puts down her phone and starts to get undressed. The sleeves feel tight around her wrists; she unbuttons her shirt and pulls it off. Then she undoes her bra, lifts up her hips from the sofa and peels off her tights. She gathers the nylon in one hand, clenching and releasing it. Her heart is pounding in her ears. She wants to have a good relationship with Helene, she really does, but it's as if they can't agree on what a good relationship means. Helene has clear demands, and seems to believe they're justified, but it doesn't feel right for Karin to give in to these demands purely and simply to be close to her. For example, she can't remember the last time Helene called just to have a chat; there are always specific things she wants Karin to make a decision about: babysitting, end-of-term celebrations, presents.

If Karin rings some evening she's sitting at home and Helene answers, she gives short, impatient replies, as though she's keeping an eye on a bubbling casserole or a child, something which at any minute is going to be more important than their conversation. There's something mechanical about it.

She sits like this for a while, with her knees apart and elbows pressing into her thighs, but in the end she straightens up and scratches herself under her breasts, where the skin is red from the wire in her bra. Wearing just her skirt, she gets up and turns on some lights. Her bookcase covers half a wall and she has no TV. There's a canvas safari chair on the other side of the coffee table and her exercise mat is rolled out on the floor in front of the balcony door. That's where she usually does her exercises in the afternoon while listening to the radio or watching the news on her laptop. She goes over to the kitchen, throws her tights in the bin under the sink and gets a bottle of gin out of the freezer. There are a couple of brown limes at the bottom of the fruit bowl. She throws them away too. The kitchen is the only room she completely renovated when she bought the flat, even though she doesn't particularly like cooking and mostly eats at the table in the sitting room. The building is from the late thirties, with a big backyard and bad soundproofing between the flats. From the kitchen she sometimes hears the neighbours having sex; she waits to boil the kettle or put away saucepans so she can listen. No one can see in; she can walk round the flat naked if she wants. At least, that's what the estate agent said when he showed her around thirteen years ago. Then he blushed. When she looks back at the periods of her life where she got most attention from men, they were when she was twelve or thirteen and when she was in her forties. Those two age groups mark the typical extremes of women's fertility, she thinks, and therefore also their sex appeal. The fact that the attention grows on the way in and out of this time span is like when a person is most interesting the moment they enter a room and the moment they leave it: first the unsullied possibility, then the imminent loss.

There's an old photo of Helene stuck on the fridge door. It's the only picture she has out, and it was taken in the old flat. In the picture Helene is squinting at the sun from a wicker chair on the balcony. Her singlet is rolled up to just below her breasts, revealing a soft teenage stomach with a scar from where her appendix was removed the year before, and a blue navel piercing. Karin had paid for the piercing, after Helene had nagged for months and shown her pictures of pop stars. Not long after, Karin saw her in a dance performance on market day in the city centre. There was no proper stage, just a circle of people that made room for the dancers' movements. Helene stood right at the front in a crop top, her piercing sparkling in the sun. She had just started using make-up, Karin remembers, and carried that precocious face like an egg on a spoon. She had been proud of her daughter. Several years later she asked Helene about the piercing, if she still had it, but then Helene looked at her stupidly and answered that the hole had closed up ages ago. 'Dad would never have let me do it,' she said. 'Do you remember how angry he got?'

'But you cried so much you got your way in the end.'

'That wasn't why I cried,' said Helene.

Karin takes a glass from the shelf over the sink. She pours in the gin, which has become thick from being in the freezer, and tops it up with the last drops of tonic. She also finds the remains of a bulgur salad in the fridge, takes off the cling film and carries the bowl and the glass into the sitting room. Her laptop is under a wool blanket on the sofa. She places it on her knee, balancing the salad bowl on a cushion next to her. The web address appears as soon as she types in the first letter.

She has stuck to the same dating website for many years now. The simple design suits her taste, and the men generally behave properly. She likes the opening conversations best, when the performance factor is obvious and therefore harmless. The better you get to know someone, the more difficult it is to decide when they're lying in order to look good. She has had the same profile picture the whole time, one where she's sitting on the balcony with her sunglasses on her head and a big smile. Only after a while did she notice the reflection in the window in the background, revealing that she was using a self-timer, that her smile was directed at hordes of strange men rather than at someone who had asked her to smile. She has kept it anyway.

After skimming through new messages, she watches an English documentary series that she enjoys about how various household products are made. The episode she chooses is about toothbrushes, and it takes the viewer around an unnamed factory. You can see how the machines melt plastic, shape handles and add bunches of nylon bristles to the toothbrush heads, which are then trimmed and finished off at an incredible speed. The amount of precision involved is amazing; she has to rewind several times to watch certain details again. The shots of nylon fibres being sorted by robot arms make her spine tingle. A handsome older man who works in the factory says that 'no human hands' come in contact with the brushes during the whole manufacturing process any longer. 'It's extremely hygienic,' he says, exposing his predictably white teeth. The powerful machines pound behind him, making him look soft and weak.

The next morning the snow has melted. She showers, has some fruit, and starts reading a new book on the way to work, using the receipt as a bookmark. The jewellery shop where she works is next door to a pharmacy and a cafe, and opposite a specialist cheese shop that always has too many employees there, young people with trusting expressions and rosy cheeks. After dragging the doormat outside the glass door, she hangs up her coat in the break room. She gathers her hair in a plastic clip, then changes into her work blazer and a pair of old moccasins with shiny, worn soles. The blazer is particularly unflattering, a tight-fitting polyester thing with her name pinned to the lapel, but after seven years she has got used to it. She makes some coffee and takes her cup out to the ergonomic stool behind the till. The shop forms a rectangle and has navy blue brocade-patterned wallpaper. There are large windows at the front and massive glass display cases at the back. Smaller ones stand here and there on the parquet floor. She wakes the computer from sleep mode and logs into the payment system. An odour of singed dust and detergent overpowers the smell of coffee. In recent years something has happened to her sense of smell. For example, she can no longer stand the smell of the bags in the rubbish bin. Not long ago she wrote a note about this to the cleaner who comes after closing time. The next day the note was still there. Underneath the person had added: *possible u are pregnant?*

Karin is the only full-time employee. On Thursdays, when they're open late, she's replaced by Ylva, a young part-timer who has her sister's name tattooed in fancy letters on her collarbone and synthetic hair attached to her own with clips. Ylva also works in the shop at weekends. In December they work together at the busiest times of day, which is a bit odd for both of them. If Karin reaches across Ylva's lap to get the key to the back room, Ylva jumps like mad and apologizes for being in the way but still glares as if she's been terribly inconvenienced. In the course of a day she probably has fifteen cups of tea, with sweetener she brings from home in a freezer bag. Karin has to look away so she doesn't go crazy each time Ylva counts out the small white pills with as much concentration as a newly qualified nurse.

The morning passes quickly. She reads, peels a banana, eats it and washes her hands afterwards. For lunch she has a smoothie from the cafe next door, then goes back and buys a coffee. Later she tries on some rings from a Swiss brand, promoted by an actor with pouty lips. She never seriously pictured a career for herself, or certainly not this one. Maybe she was stupid to have dropped out of university, pregnant with Helene, yet she's fine with where she has ended up. The days have a regularity she enjoys. She rarely listens to music; she usually reads novels and online newspapers or chats with men from the dating website and fixes dates she either keeps or cancels, depending on how she feels on the day. Sometimes she sees friends, old colleagues, goes to the cinema or has dinner. She has no problem finding things to talk about and is a good listener, but afterwards she often feels distorted by her own words and wishes she had stayed at home. It doesn't bother her to be alone. As long as your basic needs are covered – food, shelter, the possibility of intimacy – how much difference is there really between a good and a bad life? With this insight it seems embarrassing to throw yourself passionately into things, behaving like you can't distinguish between who you are and the role you play.

It wasn't planned, of course. Karin was fairly sure she didn't want children – or rather, as sure as you can be in your teens – but when she started at university, she felt like an outsider among her peers. They all seemed able to fit into social and academic situations with the utmost ease. She was always hesitant. Her personality lost its form, and that made her extra aware of everything her body did. She would only go running after dark, and buy food she didn't feel guilty about. She once went to a party, had too much to drink, and woke up on the floor with an embroidered cushion wedged under her hips, while a guy she didn't know was having sex with her from behind. She saw him later at the library. He came over and gave her a hug, as if they'd had a lovely evening. She didn't understand how anything worked. More and more she would catch herself observing people, listening to them talk, and think: Are they really serious about this?

She had started off doing sociology. Erik was two years older than her and in his second year of political science, but they still had a module in common. At these lectures he always sat at the back and talked a lot. He had a speech condition, pronouncing his r's with an extra puff of air that made him sound child-like, but he still expressed himself with convincing authority and his voice would carry through the room. He described a conflict as *an accumulation of contradictory narratives*. There were other things too, like the fact that he didn't break eye contact when he spoke to lecturers, and that he so casually put his arm around girls he knew. His whole being conveyed the impression of a firm handshake. Sometime in the spring she realized he was in love with her when, drunk and swaying from one leg to the other, he imitated how she fastened an elastic band round her ponytail before each lecture. It was a gesture she hadn't been aware of herself. The crucial moment came when she found out she was pregnant, when his eyes were bluer than they would ever be again and he said: 'We could make it work, I just know we could.' Everything exploded in warmth. It was like getting up from a chair and knowing exactly where she was heading. She was told life would be different, and that was all she wanted. After the birth, she touched her eyes and felt her lashes were still stiff with mascara. There hadn't even been time for it to rub off in her sweat.

—

After work she goes to a pub nearby. The beer-heavy heat overwhelms her, and she unwraps her scarf as she looks around for somewhere to sit. It's quite full. She finds a lung-shaped table next to the wall. There's a man her age sitting at the bar with his jacket on and a tartan scarf on his lap. Standing right by him is a girl with close-cropped hair and large breasts showing under a thin cotton top. Looking at her, Karin is reminded of another young woman, from a pornographic film, who also had close-cropped hair and was tied up with rope by two men. It was a man who had shown Karin the film, no doubt with certain expectations, but when the actor's breasts turned blue between the ropes, she asked the man to turn it off. The girl leans against the bar; the man holds his scarf in both hands. Something about the way they have positioned themselves, close but without seeming intimate, makes her curious about the vibe between them, who they are to each other. She gets up and goes over to the bar, stands on the man's left and chooses to wait for a few seconds when the bartender asks what she would like. The man orders two beers. He's probably in his late fifties, his nose is big and straight, and the skin hangs from his cheekbones like a sand dune. She likes that.

The bartender comes back with two beers and a card machine. The man looks confused. 'I've got cash,' he says, taking a crumpled five-hundred-kroner note from his breast pocket. He pulls at it with both hands.

The girl takes a big sip and wipes the froth off her lips with the back of her hand. The man surveys the room, apparently more nervous than inquisitive. He looks Karin in the eye and nods slightly. She orders a glass of wine but has to wait while the bartender opens a new bottle.

'It's pretty packed in here,' she hears the man say to the girl. His voice is warm and husky. 'Not just old fogies like me.'

'Are you okay, Dad?' says the girl.

'Splendid,' says the man.

When the change comes, he gives one of the notes from the paltry pile to his daughter.

'This can't look good,' she laughs. 'A man in a pub giving money to a younger woman.'

'Well, you certainly came cheap,' he says.

Karin carries her glass of wine back to the table. She takes her book out of her bag, glancing up now and then to observe the couple at the bar. When the daughter leaves, about an hour later, the man comes over to Karin.

'I've had a couple of beers now, so maybe it's okay to ask if I can join you?'

'Okay for you or okay for me?' she says, but she has already closed the book on her lap.

It's easy for them to chat to begin with. The conversation topics come naturally but are largely impersonal. He just can't understand how he hasn't met her earlier, he says, seeing as they are both regulars. He tells a complicated story about the owner of the place, and when he finally gets to the punchline it's so vile that she laughs extra loud, mostly because she's surprised.

Later, they go back to his place. She says yes mostly because she doesn't want to say no, and there is nothing in between for her. The weekend has also left her with a fragility she hopes to shake off. He gets two bottles of beer from the fridge and opens them with his lighter. On the worktop, there are several fresh herb plants that have been taken out of their plastic wrapping and put in individual pots. This surprises her. It doesn't go with the rest of the picture. They sit down on the sofa in the sitting room. His hair flops over his forehead each time he leans across the low table to flick ash off his cigarette. He asks if she works. She looks at him with raised eyebrows, fearing something has collapsed inside her overnight. 'I'm the manager of a jewellery shop,' she says. 'Do *you* work?'

He smiles, studying her attentively. 'Now and then,' he says.

He's a translator. After living hand-to-mouth for many years and a long period in Chile, something to do with a girlfriend, he started to translate books from Spanish to Norwegian. Now he's quite highly regarded in cultivated circles, and once he was interviewed about his job in the paper.

'They took my picture and stuff,' he says.

She looks around the room. 'But where are all your books?'

'It's like what they say about gynaecologists, I guess,' he says. 'Occupational hazard.'

He asks about her job, and the fact that he seems interested in it makes her want to tell him more about herself, so he understands her career is a result of indifference, not intellectual deficiency.

'Work to live, not the other way round?' he says, and again she feels misunderstood.

Just after they have opened their third beer, Karin hears her phone ringing in her bag on the floor. She considers not answering it at first – his hand is on her thigh, and now and then he draws small circles with his index finger from her knee up to the bottom of her skirt, possibly a memory from an earlier relationship – but she does so anyway. It's Helene. It's past ten.

'Are you at home?' says Helene. There's something off about her voice, the smoothed and softened consonants.

'Right now, you mean?'

'Yes, now. I thought I'd drop by.'

'Drop by? Why?'

The man has removed his hand, but in a warm and accommodating way. He leans forward to reach his cigarettes.

'I just want to talk,' says Helene. 'Can't you just say yes or no?'

'I'm at a friend's place,' says Karin. 'But I can meet you some-where.'

She gives her the name of the bar they just left and says she can be there in half an hour. When they have hung up, she turns to the man to explain, but he's already understood everything.

'I have a daughter of my own,' he says. 'I know how it is.'

Helene is sitting at a table at the back of the pub with a glass of white wine in front of her. She looks up and meets Karin's eye, making Karin immediately feel self-conscious. Over at the table she remains standing with her hands on the back of the chair. She says hi and asks if Helene has been waiting long. Her glass is half empty.

'Hope I didn't ruin your evening,' Helene says. 'Were you with a man?'

Karin shakes her head. 'Don't worry about it. You want an-other drink?'

Helene looks down at the stem of the glass she's holding with both hands. Her hair is subtly dyed, champagne blonde with dark shading at the roots. 'I've got one,' she says.

Karin goes over to the bar and comes back with a gin and tonic and a glass of water. A Bob Dylan song is playing in the background. The chair legs scrape on the floor when she sits down at the table. 'Oops,' she says.

'Endre's been having an affair,' says Helene. She fishes around with two fingers in the fresh glass of water for ice cubes she can put in her wine, then she takes a big sip, letting the ice cubes clink together in her mouth before spitting them back into the wine glass. 'Affair,' she says again. 'Do people still say that?'

It must be the first time in ten years Karin has seen her drunk.

'It's been going on for ages,' Helene continues. 'A year or

more, since Lea was a baby. He says he doesn't love her, that's the worst thing.'

Karin tries to absorb the information fast enough to react naturally, doing her best to look empathetic. She doesn't know what to say. For a few moments she just sits there contemplating her own inadequacy. 'Isn't it better that he doesn't love her?' she says finally.

Helene knocks back her wine and brusquely stands up. It was obviously the wrong thing to say.

'Are you leaving?' says Karin.

'No, but you can go if you want.'

'But I just got here.'

'I'm going to get another drink.'

Helene comes back with two slim glasses in her hand. 'Gin and tonic,' she says, putting down one of the glasses in front of Karin. 'Isn't that what you drink?' She sticks her nose into the glass until her cheeks touch the side. 'It smells of fir trees – does it remind you of something?'

'But you've been happy together, haven't you?'

Helene smiles. 'You must be loving this.'

'What do you mean?'

'You've been wanting to put a spanner in the works right from the beginning.'

It takes a few seconds before Karin catches the sting in what she's saying. Only then does she realize why Helene rang her. It's not support she needs but someone to blame. 'That's not true,' says Karin. 'I only want what's best for you.'

'Don't you remember how you reacted the first time I told you about Endre, after we'd moved in together? "Have you really thought about this?" That was the only thing you wanted to know. You didn't ask a single question about him. For God's sake, Karin.'

'I must have thought it all went a bit fast. You were young. You'd just come back from your year in England. I didn't understand why you suddenly rang Erik wanting money to do up that place.'

'Did Dad tell you that?'

'Yes.'

It goes quiet.

'You're pale,' says Karin.

'It's November,' says Helene.

The bartender comes over, lights the tea lights on the table with a long stem lighter and an irritating attempt at discretion. At the table where Karin sat earlier in the evening, there's a young couple in their outdoor clothes, looking tense. She gets up to go to the toilet. She looks at herself in the mirror for some time, dries her hands with paper towels and combs her hair with her fingers.

When she comes back, Helene has her hands deep inside an enormous handbag she has dumped on the table. She doesn't look up, just continues to rummage around in the bottom of the bag, as if she's searching for cutlery in a sink full of dirty water.

For Karin it's a chance to look at her. It's something she misses, that unrestricted gaze. When Helene was a teenager and still spent alternate weekends at her place, she used to borrow clothes before she went out with friends. All my stuff's at Dad's, she'd moan, then go through Karin's wardrobe with jutting-out hips and a sceptical look on her face. If she found something she liked, a dress for example, she wouldn't be embarrassed to change, exposing underwear that disappeared up her bottom and examining herself intimately in the mirror, oblivious to her mother watching from the bed. Karin was secretly moved by Helene's natural self-confidence.

'I want you to read something,' says Helene. She has shoved

her bag to one side and is reaching across the table with her lit-up phone. 'It's texts Endre has sent to his girlfriend. Read them.'

Karin takes the phone and looks hesitantly at the speech bubbles. 'Is it his phone? Why have you got it?'

'He gave it to me.'

She stares into Helene's eyes. 'Why did he do that?' she says finally. 'Are you sure they're real?'

'Yeah. He was the one who suggested it. He says it can work as – what did he call it? A kind of catharsis for us both.'

Karin looks at her. It's impossible to tell if Helene is overrun by her emotions or detached from them. 'I still don't think it's right that I read them,' she says. 'Can't you just tell me more about what's happened?' She tries to hand back Endre's phone but Helene doesn't move, just crosses her arms and leans back in her chair.

After a while Karin puts the phone between them on the table, where it lies until the screen goes black and the hearts disappear. Then Helene starts talking.

Endre had met his lover at a meditation retreat outside Stockholm, where she worked as a yoga instructor. It was the second year in a row that he had been there to cleanse his head and body from 'toxic influence', a vague umbrella term he insisted did not involve Helene and the children but rather reflected 'the general noise level in society'. When she was pregnant with Aldo, he had dabbled in Buddhism, she says, burned incense and meditated, but never quite managed to commit to it. Maybe because he was basically neurotic and it was difficult for him to embrace this idea of dissolving in an eternal stream of energy. The fact Helene has found a husband who resembles Erik – at least as far as the need for self-assertion is concerned – is annoying, but it isn't anything Karin dwells on, especially since Endre seems better able to keep people interested, even if it's only because he is more ambitious for himself than for his family. If Karin has problems with Endre, it's first and foremost because she doesn't believe he's for real, or perhaps she doesn't believe Helene is being real when she's with him. They hide behind roles that are no doubt complementary and beneficial but which make it practically impossible for Karin to spend time with them. If Helene wants Endre to do something he's basically sceptical about, she strokes the back of his neck in a phoney performance of female cunning. At such times Karin just stares at Helene and thinks: Where are you, where are you, where are you?

After the fourth round of drinks they order food from the bar, tepid snacks they eat with their fingers and which weaken the buzz that has grown in step with the alcohol. Two men at a nearby table keep glancing round, but Karin avoids their eyes.

Helene strips the meat off the chicken wings with her front teeth, piling the bones into a grotesque tower on the napkin beside the plate. 'Shall I tell you how I found out?' she says, without waiting for an answer. 'I overheard him call her Lotto when he was talking about the retreat to Lars-Erik at a dinner. And Lars-Erik – you've met him, he was Endre's best man – he knew full well who he meant, he didn't ask "Who's Lotto?" when Endre related some fact or other about raw veganism that came from her.'

'That doesn't necessarily mean anything,' says Karin. 'He's talked about the retreat before, hasn't he?'

'No, no, you don't get it. She's called Charlotte.' Helene raises her eyebrows. When she doesn't get any response, she sighs and goes on. 'Lotto is a nickname. He's always said Charlotte to me.'

'I don't know, Helene. Maybe they're just good friends. What did the messages actually say?'

'That he'd like to come inside her.'

—

The first time Karin met Endre he had already proposed to Helene. They had met in Bergen, where he was studying law, and Helene had started and dropped various humanities subjects, which in the end led to a degree in European Studies. With her ring finger hooked between two buttons on his shirt in triumphant intimacy, she said that Endre had called Erik first to ask for his permission. The way she told this revealed that she was proud he had made this old-fashioned gesture. In their wedding speeches, both had used variations on the metaphor 'coming home' about meeting the other.

Karin rarely saw them in the years that followed. In the beginning Endre seemed to like her; he asked her questions that showed he was interested and smiled warmly after hugging her. But at some stage or other he became cooler. Either it was because Helene had told him her version of a number of events, or because he no longer saw the point in making an effort when it became clear Karin wasn't central in Helene's life. At the same time as they announced the first pregnancy, they bought a large semi-detached house at Marienlyst in Oslo, with Erik's mother's inheritance and Endre's generous new salary as legal director in the Norwegian division of a Russian oil company. Just after Aldo turned two, when Helene was pregnant for the second time, without warning Endre resigned from his job. Together with a childhood friend he developed a digital platform intended to 'humanize internet shopping', and when they sold the company soon after, they used the profits to finance the development of an app to revolutionize the cleaning industry. It was the start of what Helene now dismisses as his 'nearly midlife crisis'. Endre had always loved design and could easily spend tens of thousands of kroner on a pouffe, yet recently he had started wearing a uniform consisting of khaki trousers, flannel shirts and fleece waistcoats: expensive, functional leisurewear with chunky logos that possibly had some kind of significance in his world, but which embarrassed Helene when they went to restaurants or to see friends. It didn't help either that he had stopped eating meat, corn, lactose and sugar, and underwent week-long fasts which gave him a headache and a polished glow to his face. Endre, Helene says, who had never been especially sensitive, would now cry at YouTube videos about homeless war veterans being washed and cared for by young beauticians wanting to give them back their dignity.

'He says he's moved by the thought of catharsis,' says Helene.

'What does he mean by catharsis?' asks Karin.

It takes several seconds for Helene to answer. 'I don't know. The only example he can give me is the feeling he gets after a tough workout, when he's really knackered and then takes a cold shower. But if I ask why he can't just run and shower instead of spending so many weeks a year at these weird retreats, he accuses me of ridiculing the spiritual dimension of his needs. As if I'm the selfish one.' A bartender disappears with their plates. After a pause, Helene says she has wondered if she's given Endre too much 'on an emotional level'. That it's like faking orgasms: if you fake them often enough your partner will soon find it more meaningful when you don't orgasm than when you do, and then all that is real and authentic will seem like a minus.

'I think everyone feels like that,' says Karin. 'That things haven't quite worked out as planned.'

Helene fiddles with her watch as though she's trying to break out of handcuffs. 'But what do they do then?' she says. 'Rub everything out and start again?'

—

Helene is wobbly when they stand up to leave. The last half an hour she's nearly stopped talking completely. Karin helps her into a taxi. She asks her to send a message the next day, and Helene nods vaguely. Her thighs are flat against the seat, not crossed like they usually are, and her body sways slightly, like an underwater plant. On the way home in her own taxi, Karin considers asking the driver to turn round and drive her back to the translator's, but she doesn't. It's almost three in the morning and the taste of meat and alcohol sticks to her tongue. The driver changes the music, looking at her in the mirror as if to check it's all right. She smiles back. Her eyes ache, yet she's worried she won't be able to get to sleep. If she lies awake at night, she sometimes pictures Helene's life with Endre. Each situation lies on top of the previous one like a pile of overhead transparencies, until everything becomes black and chaotic.

She recalls episodes when she has seen them together while not actually being there to affect the mood. At Endre's thirty-fifth birthday party a few years ago, she got caught in a tedious conversation with an old university friend of his who had specialized in copyright and then worked for a large international production company. He went on in detail about one specific lawsuit regarding a popular Scandinavian TV series he assumed she was familiar with. Finally she sneaked away, with the excuse that she needed a glass of water – if she'd said wine he would have offered to get some for her – and when she went into the kitchen, a big room with granite-grey cupboards and dark slate tiles on the floor, Endre stood bent over Helene, who was leaning backwards against the worktop looking radiant. The fridge door was open and Endre had his fingers in her hair. Helene seemed happy and relaxed. Then she caught sight of Karin and straightened herself up with an embarrassed smile. 'Karin,' she said.

Endre turned round and laughed when he saw her standing there in the doorway. He kissed Helene tenderly on the forehead before picking up his wine glass from the side and going back to the party. The rest of the evening, she stood watching the interaction between them with an intensity that grew in proportion with her drinking. Wherever they were in the room, they found each other with their eyes. When the copyright specialist asked her what she was looking at, she answered honestly: 'I don't know.'

Karin wakes up with a headache. She's standing in front of the basin in the bathroom, with an index finger under the cooling jet of water and two ibuprofen on her tongue, when she hears her phone vibrating on top of the washing machine. She swallows the pills and washes her face in the cold water. Her bathroom is small and white, with a window that lets in light so she can have real plants in there. She looks at her phone. *A beer tonight, same place?* it says. She answers: *Who is this?*, even though she knows. It vibrates almost immediately. *Torstein*, he writes, *the slightly debauched bloke you went home with yesterday*, and then a smiley with a dash for a nose. She writes back that she'd love to have a beer, but asks if they can see each other the day after instead; she needs a day to recover, though she doesn't write that. *Deal*, he answers. For a moment she has second thoughts, remembering the wrinkled five-hundred-kroner note, but she pushes away the image.

She orders noodle soup for lunch at work and has it delivered to the shop by a pink courier. She eats quickly, gets greasy marks on her cheeks and feels heavy and lethargic afterwards. She doesn't feel like reading. With the volume on her computer turned right down, she watches videos friends and acquaintances have shared on Facebook. In one of them a

Peruvian toddler is dancing seductively in his nappy. To manage the tiredness she buys double cappuccinos at the cafe next door, scoops up the foam with her finger and pokes the tip of her tongue under the part of the nail where it tastes bitter. She thinks about last night, about Helene, and can't remember the last time they talked like that. Not that Karin said so much, but Helene's desire to tell her was surprising, more surprising than Endre's affair. Her vulnerability made Karin want to touch her, comfort her physically, but the nearest she got was helping her out of the bar. Helene had probably started drinking long before she rang her.

Two young boys come into the shop. They have thin jackets on and their backpacks hang too far down. Karin keeps an eye on them while they look in the display cases, mumbling to each other. 'Are you looking for anything special?' she says.

They're trying to find Christmas presents for their girlfriends, says one of them; they each have three hundred kroner to spend. She shows them the few things they have in that price range, but nothing is to their liking. They leave without saying thank you.

After they have left, she has an idea and goes to Endre's Facebook page. In his profile picture he's standing in front of a cairn on a mountain plateau, smiling. He has heather round his feet and marks round his eyes from his sunglasses. The last few months he's been sharing videos and links more often than before, including an Australian research report connecting lactose with Alzheimer's and ADHD. Further down Karin finds a link to the meditation retreat in Sweden. Endre encourages his friends to go, calling the experience *hands down the coolest introspective journey* he's been on. She clicks on the link and the website she comes to is surprisingly old-fashioned, with low-resolution images and generic fonts. The banner picture shows a seated red-haired woman folded over her outstretched legs, and in the background there are two men smiling in white shirts. She scrolls down. The benefits of silent meditation, or *being in silence*, as they call it, are listed in a column of bullet points, and include everything from improved sleep and concentration to improved empathy. It also says that after only a week many will feel that time becomes irrelevant. To reach this point, you must let go of your personal life story, or at least renounce your ownership of certain elements. In so far as there is a goal for the retreat, *an intention*, it is this: the admission to an empty inner space. With her hangover like a tight elastic band around her head, Karin pictures this space. What she sees resembles an old advert she remembers from the TV, where nubile women swam in a pool filled with a zero-calorie fruit drink.

Further down there are photos of the premises. She rolls her stool nearer the screen. The main building is a large one-storey house made of blonde wood, with inlaid glass panels replacing whole walls and parts of the roof. Some smaller buildings made of the same materials prove to be living accommodation with bunk beds and room for up to eight participants. According to the caption, the bathrooms are equipped with botanical care products produced by a Swedish supermodel Karin remembers from the eighties. For a while she moves the mouse aimlessly round the archaic homepage. There's something strangely fetishistic about the whole thing in all its simplicity. It also seems paranoid; several linked articles claim they can prove a conspiracy between corrupt Western states and major food manufacturers. She tries to imagine Endre meditating on a mat or queueing to receive a bowl of nettle soup, which it says they serve, and is surprised by how easily he fits into the mental picture. It confirms what she has long believed, that he lacks substance.

She keeps checking her phone for messages but doesn't hear anything from Helene. It may be a good sign, she doesn't know. She goes onto Helene's Facebook and Instagram profiles, but they look normal. The only thing is that she hasn't posted any new pictures since the summer holiday in Italy which, in contrast, she documented fully. In one picture she's posing with Endre in front of a wall covered in climbing roses. In another she's sitting on a chair looking out over the sea and sky, which is flaming orange. Her neck is long and slender beneath a straw hat. Endre must have taken it. The truth is that Karin had never nourished the slightest hope for the person Helene would end up with one day, so it's not disappointment she feels. She's just worried Helene has drifted a long way from her true self. Or worse: that she has headed there intentionally.

After work she takes the bus home. She tries to look out of the window but just meets her own reflection. Her features stand out in clear patches on the glass, like an after-image against the thickening darkness outside. In the accordion-like section of the bus there's a man standing in a fur-lined parka talking loudly on his phone. He says he has the whole organization against him but that he's 'always been an underdog'. In front of her there's a woman with a little girl on her lap, and she's plaiting her hair with nimble fingers. Personally, Karin always hated having her hair plaited as a child. She remembers the pulling on her scalp, her mother's hand appearing over her shoulder, silently requesting the elastic band back. As soon as Karin was old enough to refuse, her mother made a point of swapping their roles. 'Can you brush my hair?' she would ask, just because she enjoyed being cared for.

Asking to have your desires satisfied like that is unthinkable for Karin. The world becomes hard and cold when she imagines everyone going round demanding pleasure. To her, nothing feels good unless it's initiated by others, and even then she's troubled by the thought of having to return the favour.

Her mother was thirty-six when she had her. Before she met Karin's father she had been married to a Swedish architect she met at a mountain cabin in Rondane just after the war. They never had children; they tried, but when it didn't work out her mother assumed there was something wrong with her. Before she married Karin's father she had told him she couldn't get pregnant, but that didn't seem to bother him. 'He insisted that it was only me he wanted,' her mother said.

The conversation took place one summer many years ago. Her mother was in her mid-sixties and single. She had borrowed her brother's cottage while he was in Greece with the family, and Karin had driven down there to spend a few days with her. They planted a herb garden behind the cottage as a thank you, or for something to do. While they worked, her mother kept bringing up Karin's father, who had remarried a long time ago. She praised him with a look of defiance, clearly enjoying the role as the tolerant heroine – hurt but upright – even in front of Karin, although she could have just as well been honest with her.

'The fact he accepted me so completely made me feel whole,' her mother said. 'Sometimes I think that's what helped me finally get pregnant, after all those years… I was always so tense with Bo.'

Her mother took off one of her gardening gloves and drank up the juice on the paving stone beside her. The self-indulgent look on her face made Karin squirm; it made her irritable and condescending, even though she had promised herself to be nice. 'Or maybe it was Bo who couldn't have children,' she said. 'Isn't that more likely?'

Her mother pressed her lips together and suddenly smiled. 'Your father could be very romantic, you know. When we came home from a party, he always whispered "I'm so glad we have each other" before he fell asleep. And he used to…' She giggled, laying her hand on Karin's bare shoulder.

'Mother, we don't need to talk about this,' said Karin. She always got the feeling of letting herself down when she allowed her mother to take her into her confidence. It was a struggle to keep enough distance to be able to breathe. She had heard it all before, anyway.

'I thought you'd like to hear about how nice it could be between us,' said her mother. She looked hurt, pulled on her glove again and started to dig around the rosemary roots with a teaspoon. Under a snug T-shirt, her stomach bulged over the top of her shorts, accentuated with a much-too-tight belt. Karin knew exactly what she looked like beneath her clothes; she knew how her pubic hair grew in stiff clumps towards the middle, knew the whitish-yellow skin on the back of her heels that she tried her best to file away with pumice stone in the shower. The problem was that her mother had a narrative about herself that stretched reality into something Karin couldn't accept. Karin often felt obliged to contradict her, for no other reason than to create a shared reality, a room in which they could agree that the floor was the floor and the ceiling was the ceiling, but her mother refused and resisted. It meant that Karin either gave in, acknowledging and therefore reinforcing her mother's myths, or took up the fight armed with 'how things really were'. Only in the first scenario did she ever feel appreciated.

Soon after she turned sixty-six, her mother had a massive heart attack. In the months after the funeral, Karin couldn't let go of the images from that weekend at the cottage. Once they had finished the herb garden, they had gone down to the fjord to swim. Her mother swam naked; she stood on the sandy sea-bed screwing up her eyes, the bottle of shampoo floating in the water beside her. She washed her hair twice to make enough foam, closed her eyes tight again and dipped under to rinse it off. Karin sat on a towel on the sloping rocks watching her. Her mother's body floundered under water, then she popped up with a gasp in circles of soap and asked: 'Is it all out?'

Back home she turns on the lights one by one, crossing the floor with familiar strides. She bought the flat with money she inherited from her mother. It has four rooms, including a spare room furnished with a single bed, a desk she should have thrown out ages ago, and a framed art poster on the wall. She's glad she lives alone. She likes the way things look. When the sun comes in at the right angle, the sitting room becomes swathed in a golden light that makes the piles of books and flowers in vases resemble a still life.

For supper she makes soup. On the days she doesn't binge, which she normally does a couple of times a week, she eats very little. It's an eating pattern that works well, and which she's happy with. She hears wardrobe doors being pushed open and shut by her neighbour. She switches on the radio and finds the channel with classical music. When she peels the onion, the outer layer pierces the skin under her nail, and with her finger in her mouth and tongue against the cut, she is seized by a slackness that overpowers her almost like sleep. She opens the window and lets in the cold air. At first she tries not to drink, but then she fills a glass with red wine from the box on the kitchen shelf while the soup simmers.

Afterwards she showers, washes her hair and scrubs herself thoroughly with an exfoliating mitt. Her skin glows red in the full-length mirror on the bathroom door. She moisturizes her body with lotion, puts on her dressing gown and sits down on the sofa with her laptop. The warmth from the computer spreads to her thighs and she places a cushion between them. She's about to go onto the dating website, but instead clicks on Endre's Facebook profile again. Among his friends she finds two women called Charlotte, but it's easy to guess which one it is. In her profile picture she's sitting at the end of a pier in burgundy yoga pants. In the section where she presents herself Karin finds a link to a blog. The page she clicks to is feminine and modern. A photo gallery shows Charlotte in various meditative yoga positions in a lush woodland area, encircled by birch trunks. Her body is hard and smooth like technology, in contrast to all the nature around. In a section encouraging the reader to *get to know* her, it says she runs a *wellness community of like-minded people* focusing on *intensive introspection practice*. She dreams of this becoming a mass movement. As a child she struggled with food allergies and asthma, she writes, but in her teenage years she had a *predestined meeting* with an Ayurvedic doctor at a market, and since then has been a raw vegan. It's as if she *has had a tap containing infinite cosmic energy installed in her chest*; she wakes up *euphoric* each morning. Below, Karin finds the video of a lecture filmed at a Finnish meditation conference.

The video begins with the sound of clapping coming to an end. Charlotte is standing on the stage with her palms pressed together in front of her chest. She's wearing a short yellow dress and sandals with tanned leather straps in a delicate T over the instep. She seems to be in her early forties. The subject of the lecture is boundaries, she says. She wants to know if she's not the only one who struggles to set them. The camera sweeps over nodding faces in the room. Karin freezes the picture but doesn't see Endre.

'On the one hand it's about eliminating expectations,' she says. 'Not being disappointed when a child or a friend or a lover doesn't act the way we want. At the same time' – she raises her hand – 'without expectations we lose our boundaries. And we need boundaries. Anything else is anarchy.'

The microphone she has taped to her cheek crackles. She addresses the invisible 'you' beside her, adopting a more ped-agogical tone. 'I accept that *you* don't act the way I want, that *you* don't answer my texts. That's your choice. I want you to be your true, *authentic* self. But I like getting answers to my texts, so if you don't answer me, I'm going to spend less time with you. Maybe' – at this point she pauses and raises her eyebrows – 'no time at all.'

It's a long video; Karin fast-forwards back and forth. Towards the end of the lecture, Charlotte squats at the edge of the stage with her weight on her heels and her thighs squeezed together so you can't see her underwear. Her eyes glow with an intense heat.

'Because if you don't look after yourself,' she says, shaking her head, as if the thought itself fills her with more distress than she can bear, 'who will?'

After work the next day Karin goes to meet Torstein. It's raining, and she looks down while she walks so her make-up doesn't run. There's something about him she can't figure out. She has a feeling he took something from her; she can't put her finger on what it is, she just knows she wants it back.

He's sitting at the same table as last time, against the wall. He has two glasses of beer in front of him, one half empty. When he sees her coming, he nudges the full glass across the table towards her, as if it will tip over the edge if she doesn't hurry up. She responds by taking the first sip standing up, then pulls off her coat and sits down, with him watching her closely the whole time. The chair is made of heavy wood, upholstered in leather with a web of white veins from overuse. She places her arms awkwardly on the armrests, like she's some kind of emperor.

'Should I have got up?' he says.

'No,' she says.

'But then I don't get a kiss.'

'No.'

He smiles and asks how she is. She answers, then they drink quickly. This time he tells her more about his life, she doesn't need to ask. He was born in Stavanger, he says, but moved to Oslo when he was eleven. His father worked as an architect, his mother was a graphic artist and art reviewer in the paper. She suffered from migraines and eating disorders his whole childhood. 'She was one of the first in Norway to be fed by tube,' he says, as if it's a sporting achievement.

After devouring Hemingway at an early age, he decided to write 'the great Norwegian novel', and took casual work to get by while he wrote. When he came back from Chile – a trip he doesn't tell her much about, other than that he caught a stomach virus that nearly killed him – he persuaded an old friend who worked as an editor at a big publishing house to let him have a go at translating. On his trip he had discovered a Chilean novelist, or rather he had *read* his work; the young Chilean already had cult status in his homeland thanks to a series of surrealistic murder mysteries which many, but not Torstein, read as political allegories. The translation was well received and he continued. Since then he has translated almost forty books, he reckons, and some of them he's really proud of.

'I work when it suits me, from wherever I want, and earn just what I need. Paradoxically, it's given my life structure,' he says. He lays his hands down on the table in front of him. His wrists are strong, with blue lines under the skin leading out to his fingers. His waxed jacket is hanging over the back of his chair. She goes across to the bar and orders again, red wine for herself and beer for him, then pays by card.

'What about the book you were going to write?' she says. 'The great Norwegian one?'

He laughs. 'No, nothing came of that, luckily.' He takes a swig of beer. His sweater is so worn at the elbows, she can see through to his checked shirt. 'Well, not luckily, that was a stupid thing to say. Who knows, maybe I was on to something for a while. But I do feel like the books I've translated are mine.'

Anyway, if it hadn't been for his job he wouldn't have met his ex-wife, he says. One of his translations was going to be performed as a play, and he helped adapt the book for the stage.

'I actually did a lot of the work, even though I wasn't credited in the programme,' he says.

At that time his ex-wife worked as a carpenter making props, and the two of them got chatting during one of the rehearsals. It was impossible not to notice her, he says; she was beautiful and 'huge like an Amazon'. They soon got married, driven by a shared dream about a house in the country and children who could run around while he wrote and she made furniture, and where they could grow their own vegetables. When she became pregnant at the first attempt, they were even more convinced they were meant for each other, but a traumatic birth and subsequent complications deterred them from trying again. They bought a terraced house just outside the city centre, and even though they continued to talk about the house in the country and the children they would have there as soon as they got it all together, they stopped believing in each other.

'Without that dream we quickly drifted apart,' Torstein says. 'Now she's married to a law professor, a nice bloke, and they have two kids. More girls. Helga, my daughter, is studying marine biology in Trondheim.' He smiles. He's finished his beer and seems pleased to have made it through his story without forgetting the details he obviously enjoyed providing. Now he's looking at her. 'And what about you then? What's your story?'

'My story?'

He doesn't register her sarcastic tone of voice, or else chooses to ignore it. 'Yeah. Tell me about your life.'

'I don't know if it's a story.' She picks up her wine glass and holds it a few centimetres over the table, twirling the stem round with her fingers. 'I work in a jeweller's, didn't I tell you last time? Before that, I used to work for many years for a furniture franchise, which got closed down when the owner got breast cancer. And I'm from here, from Oslo.'

He nods, so she continues.

'My father ran a business importing fridges and freezers, and sold them to shops all over the country.' She stops, is about to take a sip, but puts down the glass instead. 'He was pretty successful for a while, I think, but then he went bankrupt, and he left my mother soon afterwards. She trained as an occupational therapist and got a job at a day centre.'

'Do you have happy memories?' he says.

She laughs, hoping to embarrass him, but he keeps looking at her with the same enigmatic expression until she breaks eye contact. She can remember that her mother played compilation albums of classical music at the weekends, that she made soft-boiled eggs and cut stems on the kitchen worktop and arranged flowers in sculpted glass vases. She remembers that her father peed sitting down, with the door open, that he went running every day after work and left stubble in the basin which she had to rinse away every morning before she brushed her teeth. If he got angry or overwrought, he often slapped her on the top of her head, a hard thud, as if he was pounding the roof of a car. She remembers an incident at the dinner table when she was small. Her mother was in a particularly good mood and was telling a long-drawn-out story. Her father remained silent, but at one point, while her mother was still talking, he got up from the bench, walked round the table to where her mother was sitting, and gave her a long, hard kiss. From where Karin was sitting she could see his tongue twisting in her mother's mouth. She remembers it lasting ages. Afterwards he carried his plate calmly over to the worktop as though nothing had happened, then went into the sitting room to read and listen to music while he waited for his coffee. Karin remembers the expression on her mother's face, caught somewhere between pride and horror. She had told this story to people she wanted to get closer to, always testing the waters. It was easy to assume the memory appeared suddenly and came gushing out before she knew it, and that made the listener – usually a man – feel special, and made the content seem titillating. For Karin it was like sharing a confidence, without understanding what she was trying to reveal. The reactions were many and varied, few of them satisfactory. The last man she had told made a stupid face and praised the parents for showing phys-ical love in her presence. His misinterpretation provoked her, but at the same time made her doubt what she had seen.

'I don't remember that much,' she says finally. 'But yes, mostly.'

'When did it happen?' says Torstein.

'When did what happen?'

'How old were you when they separated?'

'Ten, eleven.' She goes quiet. The way he listens makes her feel insecure. It's as though he's absorbing every word, and she's worried the substance will drift out of her reach.

'And you have a daughter,' he says, as if to get her started again.

'Yes. Helene. She's married and has two children, but I don't see them very often.'

He nods. 'But it was her you were going to see the other evening?'

'Yes, she needed help with something.'

'That's nice,' he says. 'That she comes to you.'

She doesn't know what to answer. She senses that the memory of her parents is getting mixed up with the relationship he imagines she has with Helene and the relationship they actually have, and that it's wrong; she can't work out how she'll be able to separate all the parts again. She suggests they go back to his place.

Back at Torstein's she sits down on the sofa like last time. There's a smell of ash from the wood-burning stove in the corner. While he fetches the wine, she has a look round the sitting room. The flat is quite big, with an open-plan kitchen. The floor is worn and there's old fibreglass wallpaper; but the lamps and furniture are nice and in good condition, except for the sofa cover, which has small threads coming out of it and dark stains, maybe coffee, on one of the cushions. Above the TV there's a framed film poster, with the title in blood-red letters. The picture shows a blonde woman in a bath holding a paperback. She's looking up quizzically at a man in a hat who is sitting on the side of the tub, clothed. The man seems about to say something, but he's staring ahead at nothing in particular. From where she's sitting on the sofa, Karin feels like both the wondering woman and the man with his eyes somewhere else.

'Have you seen it?' Torstein says, nodding at the poster.

He comes over to the sofa with two full wine glasses. The

corner of the rug is overturned, exposing the anti-slip underlay. She shakes her head.

'You should. You'd like it, a stylish woman like you. Bardot sunbathing naked with a book on her behind, that's you, you know.' He laughs. 'I've got it here, we can watch it together one evening.'

She frowns, taking the glass he hands her. They sit there with their thighs touching. He continues talking about the film, about the Italian island where the story is set. At one point she moves position, nestling her back against the arm of the sofa, and then he leans forward and lifts her feet onto his lap. Her socks are edged with dust and baggy around the toes.

'You're a bit like Bardot yourself, you know,' he says, his eyes wandering over her face appreciatively. 'With that blonde hair and those lips.'

He massages her heels with both hands, and kneads the soles of her feet with his knuckles. It could have been pleasant, but her underarms are sticky and her ankles itch. She pulls up her legs to scratch them. The movement is sudden, a little too sudden perhaps, as he looks surprised but doesn't say anything. Then he reaches for his glass of wine and knocks back half of it in one go.

'I watch quite a lot of films,' he says. 'I've borrowed a hard disc from my daughter with loads of old stuff on it – she's good at that sort of thing. I like having something to watch. You're probably more of a reader? That's great. I remember you reading that time, in the bar. I liked that.'

'I mostly watch TV series on the internet.'

He looks at her and tuts. 'So you're one of them, are you? What are you into at the moment then?'

She's suddenly scared she's boring him. Why else talk about TV series? 'You don't need to do this,' she says.

'Do what?' he says.

'Ask me questions about myself. I don't particularly enjoy answering, so if you're doing it for my sake, you really don't need to.'

He laughs again. 'Okay. Let's say I'm doing it for my own sake then.'

His face has become a shade irritated, or maybe frustrated, slightly impatient. She realizes it's up to her to save the night, so she talks about the documentary series she likes, and the episode she saw the other day about the toothbrushes. She notices she becomes enthusiastic trying to explain as precisely as possible what it is she likes about the pictures of factories and mass production, and it feels good to articulate her thoughts to someone else.

'You see,' he says afterwards, while he strokes the hair out of her face. 'Everyone enjoys talking about themselves.'

He means well, she can see that in his eyes, but she still feels tricked. When they go into his bedroom the curtains are pulled shut. She stands there and looks around. There are books on shelves on all the walls and in piles on the floor next to the bed. He smiles, as though she's found out his secret. In a corner there's a humidifier constantly puffing steam towards the ceiling. The darkness and dampness give the room a tropical atmosphere, making it easy to imagine she's somewhere else; but it's fine to be where she is, at least until he falls asleep. Then she goes home in a taxi.

The following evenings she stays in. It's Thursday and she has gone to bed early when the phone rings. It's Helene.

'If I buy the tickets and find a hotel, can you come to London with me at the weekend?'

'London? This weekend?'

'Yeah. From tomorrow till Sunday night.'

'Why? What's going on there?'

'Nothing, well not really, but – What is it? I'm on the phone. With my mother. Yes, my mother – Karin? Karin, can you hold on a minute?' The sound becomes muffled, as if she's holding the phone against her chest.

Karin drags herself up and sits with her back against the headboard. There's a strong wind blowing outside, and the window sucks in the blind like a mouth behind a plastic bag. It makes her agitated.

'Hello? Are you still there?' Helene's voice sounds shrill. 'Sorry, it was Endre. I'm in the bedroom. He's…' The sentence is left hanging in the air.

She says she needs to get away, just for a weekend – 'nothing exotic'. She doesn't want to experience anything new, she says; that's what she wants to get away from. London is the most neutral place she can think of.

'I've got some friends there, from my exchange year, but I haven't spoken to them for ages, so as far as I'm concerned we can just go shopping and eat scones.'

'What about the kids?'

'Endre's looking after them,' she says. 'This weekend, I mean. Right now I just need some time, preferably with someone where I don't need to worry about what they're thinking.'

'And that's me?'

'You are my *mother.*'

Something stirs in Karin when she uses that word. 'Okay,' she says. 'I'll come. It'll be nice to have some time away.'

'Thanks,' says Helene, and she sounds relieved.

'I work till five, but I can ask Ylva if she can lock up for me, if you want to leave earlier?'

'No, it's fine. We can take the seven-thirty flight. We can make it if you meet me at the entrance to the airport express train just before six.'

'Yes, that's fine. That leaves me plenty of time.'

The word *time* keeps coming up, Karin notices, like a code from someone who needs to warn of a danger but can't say it out loud.

'Fine,' says Helene. She thanks her again, more formally this time. 'Thank you, Karin.'

The summer when Helene was one and Karin was still together with Erik, they hired a car and drove through Germany. They had only booked rooms in advance in a few big cities, otherwise they played it by ear; or rather, Erik had a travel guide he consulted, so it wasn't totally haphazard. He wanted to take the Romantic Road, a 350-kilometre-long stretch of southern Germany that had been given this name by desperate tour operators after the Second World War, and supposedly marked with brown signs. As soon as they reached the motorway, Karin took off her jeans and sat with her feet on the dashboard eating nuts, which she shared with Erik. She held her hand in front of his mouth like a dog bowl, so he didn't need to take his eyes off the road. It tickled when he used his tongue to dig out the last nuts. He licked off the salt with so much spit that she had to dry her palms on the car seat afterwards. 'Hey, remember it's a rental car,' he said, but with a smile.

Behind him, fastened in a patterned child seat, sat Helene with sticky thighs and bright eyes under her sun hat. Beside her there were crocheted blankets, jars of baby food, and plastic spoons stolen from petrol stations. The car bonnet sizzled in the sun. Karin rolled down the window and sliced through the air with her hand, imagining she left a gash in the landscape outside. They stopped at motels along the way, by lakes when they could.

One evening they sat next to each other on the veranda outside the motel room they had rented for the night, south of Munich. They watched a bird digging with its beak in the gravel of the car park. Karin tried to remember if that was where she had shaken the biscuit crumbs off Helene's blanket, and was struck by the short distance from where she had stood then to where she sat now. Erik held two of her fingers, pushing back the cuticles in a neurotic rhythm.

'Ow,' she said.

'Hmm?' He looked at her absent-mindedly.

She blew at her nails pointedly, then shook her fingers.

'Sorry,' he said.

There were green plants climbing up the diamond-patterned partition between the entrances to the rooms. They could hear the neighbours in the room next door whispering softly, the sharp then frothing sound of a can of beer being opened. It was an English couple in their fifties; they had met earlier when Karin sat with Helene on her lap, feeding her. Perhaps they were whispering now because of the sleeping baby. She wanted to ask them to speak louder.

'Tomorrow I thought we could have quite a long drive. Someone recommended a place right outside Füssen,' said Erik. 'There's a Bavarian castle there from the 1800s that's supposed to be worth visiting. We're up for it, aren't we?'

She didn't know if she was up for it. She thought they had been driving a long way every day. 'Can't we have another night here first?'

'Here?' Erik glanced around him, at the gravel and cracked concrete under their feet. Inside there was turquoise wallpaper and flesh-coloured tiles in the bathroom. 'This was just somewhere to stop, wasn't it?' He looked at her. 'Okay then, we'll do that. But then we leave early the day after tomorrow?'

Karin nodded.

'If I remember correctly there was a king who drowned in the lake out there. Ludwig or something.'

She had no idea what he was talking about, but she smiled. He smiled back, took her hand again and placed it on his lap. She let him hold it a while before she took it back. The whispering next door was interrupted by something that sounded like suppressed sniggers.

'Shall I get some beers from the minibar?' she asked.

'There isn't a minibar here, that was at the other place,' said Erik. He looked at his watch. 'But I can drive to the petrol station we saw on the way and buy some?'

'You don't need to,' she said.

'Yes, I'll go. It's nice sitting outside.' He got up, carefully opened the door to the dimly lit room and came out again with the car keys in his hand. 'Is there anything else you want?'

She shook her head. Before he seated himself in the car, he nodded and she nodded back, realizing at the same time that it wasn't at her but at the couple next door. She tried to get a glimpse of them between the holes in the partition wall, and saw the flame of a lighter and caught a whiff of tobacco. She got up and walked over the crunchy gravel to where they were sitting. The woman was plump with large breasts and blonde hair, a flat fringe smoothed diagonally across her forehead. Her hair stood out in matted clumps from the top of her head, like when a child has just woken up, and her arms stuck out of a sleeveless shirt. Karin smiled and asked in English if she could bum a cigarette. The woman handed her the packet and said, 'Here you go, my love.' The man immediately got up and lit her cigarette, shielding it with his hand even though it wasn't windy. He wore a Hawaiian shirt and had tattoos of dragons and daggers meandering over his leathery skin. She thanked him and took a deep drag, sensing how the lightness filled and lifted her. She hadn't smoked since before she got pregnant.

The woman introduced herself as Nicola, her husband was Hugh. They lived in Brighton and ran a clothes shop, they said, but every summer they went travelling for a whole month, usually by car. Last year they had been to Spain, but this year they had rather reluctantly come here, to Germany, to visit Nicola's younger sister, who had married an East German doctor and now lived in Munich. They had one week left of their holiday and were now going to drive around. Hugh reached for the blue cool box they had by the door, took out a beer and handed it to Karin, who took it and thanked him. They seemed to have had a lot already.

They had been married for twenty-eight years, they said, and been together for over thirty. 'We use the same toothbrush, that's the secret,' said Nicola. She laughed with a loud guffaw which made her breasts swing under her tight top.

Karin liked her.

'And we dance,' said Hugh. 'Every weekend. Lindy Hop, jive, Charleston. It keeps us active.' He winked.

Karin had another cigarette and another beer. When the hire car drove into the parking space, the headlights swept over their faces. Erik opened the car door, lighting up the inside, and she could see he was staring at the glowing dot in the darkness in front of her. He came towards them with a white carrier bag dangling at his ankles. After saying hello, he stood there as if waiting for something.

'Aren't you going to sit down?' asked Karin.

'Yeah, I'll just check on Helene first,' he said, putting down the bag on the concrete where Karin was sitting on a cushion.

She peeped inside. He'd bought a six-pack and a bag of peanuts. She stroked his almost hairless calf. 'Okay,' she said.

When he hadn't come back after a while, she went into the room. He was sitting on the bed with a book.

'You just stayed here? I thought you were going to come back out.'

'Yeah.' He closed his book. 'I just wasn't feeling very sociable.'

'But you've bought beer?'

'I thought it would just be you and me.'

'But it is, the whole time. I was just talking to the neighbours. They dance the Lindy Hop.' She wriggled her hips. He looked at her and smiled, but she realized he was ashamed. He just couldn't do it. 'Let me just go out and say goodnight,' she said. 'I'll give them two of the beers, then we can have the rest of them here in bed.'

He said she didn't need to, that she could sit up longer with them if she wanted to, but she went out and said goodnight, and the next morning it was nice to wake up with empty beer cans on the bedside table and Erik's warm, dry body next to hers.

She lifted Helene out of the travel cot and carried her into the bathroom. The fluorescent lights blinked a few times. She held Helene on her hip and spoke to their reflection.

'Look at us,' she said. They were both naked.

Later that morning Erik went for a run. Karin said he was mad to run in the heat, but he was restless, he said, and needed to stretch his legs. After Helene had gone to sleep, Karin walked around the building. She had left the window open so she could hear if she started crying. The colours of the landscape seemed as separate as crayons in a box. There were flowers growing against the wall. She picked a couple, making the palm of her hand yellow and sticky. On the other side of the motel she found Nicola. She was sitting on a deckchair reading a magazine, with a serious expression on her face. She was topless, and she had a fabric visor on her head. There was a battered paperback lying on the grass next to a bunch of red grapes arranged on folded toilet paper. Behind them was the row of windows; a TV was on, someone was in the shower. Karin spread out the motel towel on the grass, kicked off her sandals and pulled her T-shirt over her head with her arms crossed. Underneath she was wearing a swimming costume.

The front of the magazine Nicola was reading was covered with news about two celebrities, a famous musician and an actress, who had got married. Nicola held the magazine close to her face, examining the picture of the newly-weds. 'Pearls!' She shook her head. 'Isn't it strange how all these girls suddenly become so conservative when they get married? Last week I read that she was carried out of a French nightclub, cross-eyed with drink.'

She put down the magazine on her stomach, lifted the visor and smoothed back her fringe with one hand. The rushing noise from the motorway rose and fell with the passing cars. In front of them there were white clothes hanging on two drying racks. Karin recognized her underwear. They had handed in a bag of dirty clothes to the motel laundry service after agreeing to stay an extra night.

Nicola had rolled her bikini bottoms a long way down her hips. Her stomach bulged over her pelvis when she bent over to get the suntan lotion. She applied it vigorously to her shoulders and chest, then handed the bottle to Karin. 'Put lots on, you've got such lovely skin,' she said.

Karin wondered if she could hear Helene and turned towards the window to listen, but the sounds came from the TV in the room next door. Nicola stretched over for the grapes, took a couple and chewed them while she continued to study the pictures from the wedding. A double-page spread showed the bride and groom in front of a massive cake with many tiers, and a plastic figure looking just like them on the top.

Nicola wetted the tip of her finger and turned the page. 'Let me give you some advice,' she said. 'And I'm saying this as someone who's been married for nearly thirty years – just remember you can get married more than once.'

'Or not at all,' said Karin.

'But I don't advise that – at least get married once. It can be really nice, you know, being tied to someone. It's character-building. Just remember to…' She tapped her knuckles against her temple knowingly.

Karin couldn't normally stand being given advice, but now she hung on Nicola's every word because she liked hearing her talk. She made it possible to have a kind of no-ties intimacy.

'Let me put it this way,' said Nicola. 'I do a lot for Hugh, maybe a bit too much sometimes, but that's because I know exactly what's in it for me. I'm smart like that. Always have been.' When she was younger, she had enjoyed offering sex to unsuspecting men, to see their faces light up, as though she had given them the best present in the world. 'It made *me* feel fantastic, like an energy drink. Do you know what I mean?' She held together the pages of the magazine for a minute, scrutinizing Karin. 'There were no victims. Everyone was happy.'

'Was this while you were married to Hugh?'

'It was the sixties. He was happy too, I can promise you that. But now I'm past it.' With a nail she scraped off an insect struggling to fly off her smeary stomach. Then she laughed. 'The packaging isn't so appealing any more.'

When Erik came back from his run, Hugh was sitting on the veranda with Helene on his lap. He was singing Elton John's 'Tiny Dancer', moving her around like a marionette. There was an open beer can on the ground beside him. Karin could see Erik's confused reaction through the window, from where she stood inside mixing drinks. When she came out, Hugh had already explained. Erik was dripping with sweat from his run but seemed calm and cheerful, as he often did after exercising. He accepted a beer, just had to shower first. Through the partition she saw him stretching against the wall. Sweat ran from his temples and his thighs were a nutty brown, despite her saying they had spent most of the time in the car. She considered letting Nicola and Hugh look after Helene for ten minutes so she could join him in the shower, but she didn't know how she would ask them and wasn't sure how many beers Hugh had had either.

A fat yellow Labrador which belonged to the motel owners lay prostrate in the shade of the building. Nicola put down an ice-cream box full of water on the gravel, but the dog hardly managed to lift its head. She dipped her hand in the water and stroked its fur.

'Really, I'm a cat person,' she said over her shoulder. 'We've got two at home, but they're fine by themselves while we're away. Independent creatures, not like this helpless furball here.' She got up, went over to Karin and lowered herself slowly into the deckchair beside her. 'Our kids were crazy about dogs when they were small, but we absolutely refused to get one, so they went for walks with the neighbour's poodle instead. Until they lost interest, which they did, one by one.'

'Dad's got a giant schnauzer,' said Karin. She didn't know why she said it, even though it was true.

'One of those big ones? That'll be fun for your little girl when she's a bit older.'

Helene was sitting on a folded quilt in front of them, dribbling onto some toy blocks. Someone whistled from a doorway; the dog dragged itself up and lumbered off in the direction of the sound.

'How many kids do you have?' asked Karin.

'Three,' said Nicola. She followed the dog with her eyes. Two of their children worked in finance, she said, the other was studying medicine and volunteering for a year for an English health organization in Tanzania. Nicola called her naive and self-righteous, while Hugh said something about work keeping the thoughts pure. He crouched down and rummaged through an old bowling bag for cassettes he wanted to play on the tape recorder they had brought from England. Nicola slid a bare, shoddily pedicured foot under his Hawaiian shirt and up his back.

'They've got a bit hung up on therapy now they're grown up, so we don't see them that much,' said Nicola. 'But I'm sure they'll get over it sooner or later. They know what I think – I've got no patience with all of that.'

'With therapy?' said Karin.

'With blaming other people.'

Erik appeared from around the partition wall with two sandwiches in his hand. His hair hung in wet tufts against his forehead and his T-shirt had dark patches on the back where he hadn't managed to reach with the towel. He sat down next to Karin, offered her some of his sandwich and stroked her neck. His hands smelled fresh from the soap. Before the conversation warmed up, they talked about hire cars, and then the German car industry, but afterwards they just sat chatting about their lives, and although Erik didn't say much, he followed attentively, which Karin liked.

Later on, after they had put Helene to bed, Hugh was drunk and incoherent, leading Karin round on the gravel in an increasingly lecherous swing dance. Nicola came and saved her, so Karin could sit down beside Erik and drink up the rest of the gin while they watched the dancing couple. Nicola's fingers clung onto Hugh's shirt pocket. It was a version of the figures on the wedding cake Karin could live with, she thought, a version who knew they were figures, and that they stood with their feet planted in cream.

'You're drunk,' said Erik, when she tried to explain this to him before they fell asleep.

The following morning Karin knocked on the next-door window to say goodbye, but no one came. She shoved a note under the door. It was nine o'clock, and the birds were singing in the trees that cast shadows over the row of parked cars, all with splatters of white on the roof. They strapped Helene into the wobbly car seat; in an hour she would be asleep. When the car started the radio came on, and Erik turned down the volume, placed his hand behind Karin's headrest and reversed out of the motel car park on the crunchy gravel. They drove past green fields lined by trees. Erik asked what she had written on the note.

'*Enjoy the rest of your trip*, and our address.'

'Four grandchildren they don't see and they're still not remotely interested in questioning any of the choices they've made? I just don't get how anyone could be so self-centred.'

Erik changed gears, checked the blind spot and pulled out onto the motorway.

'Well, I think the children sounded quite self-centred,' she said.

He looked at her and then back at the road. 'Those two were a joke, Karin. I can't believe you don't see that.'

Somewhere or other outside Cologne, Erik proposed. It was apparently spontaneous, and he was empty-handed, but then Karin found the ring some days later, hidden in his toilet bag. It dawned on her that he had probably been planning to propose at the Bavarian castle, where she had fallen ill, and that the whole of the Romantic Road was part of a bigger plan he was revealing bit by bit. For the rest of the holiday, nothing was the same. She said yes, but he didn't believe her, and after two days of constant arguments they lost track of who really wanted what, and what a possible compromise would consist of. She was taken aback by his anger. He broke a glass and cried. At one point he reached for her neck to pull her closer, to kiss her, but she instinctively pulled away, afraid he would hurt her. It was an unfamiliar reflex that stunned them both. Still, it worked as a kind of reconciliation, a distress flare showing them where they stood in the dark.

That night she held him, stroking her hands over his hips and thighs, drawing him closer with a pure and honest desire to protect what they had. But in the morning, when he brusquely changed gears and stared at the road ahead, she looked out of the window and it felt like each section of the landscape that disappeared from sight was something she had lost out on and would miss.

While they were waiting for the ferry in Kiel, Erik got out and stretched his legs. His shorts were crumpled after the long drive and he was barefoot in his sailing shoes. She saw him walk towards the cafe with the compact elegance of an athlete. When he disappeared out of sight, she clambered over into the back seat. Helene had been whining since they left Hamburg, but now she was quiet. Karin stroked her cheek, then wiggled her finger into the corner of her mouth and let her squeeze it between her tingling gums, waiting until it hurt before she pulled it out again. Helene started to whimper immediately. Karin dangled the car keys in front of her like a rattle to calm her down. When that didn't work, she gave her the keys to play with. 'Have you had a nice time?' she whispered, but straight away felt self-conscious.

Erik could sit with Helene for hours – 'Pap-pa, mam-ma, can you say that?' – with his hand on his chest and careful diction. Personally, she couldn't. She was afraid of creating connections in that young brain that weren't right.

'You think too much,' said Erik.

He could call several times a day, often just to ask if Helene had said anything. When she answered no, Karin felt as though she hadn't done her job properly, which was partially confirmed when he asked: 'But you do talk to her, don't you?' In a book about children's language development, she had read that it was a good idea to repeat key words, for instance: 'Where's Daddy? Has Daddy gone out? There's Daddy' and so on. Now, sitting in the back seat, she had a go herself, pointing at the figure on the way back to the car and saying: 'There's Daddy. Can you see Daddy? There's Daddy.'

'Daddy,' said Helene.

Karin could hardly believe it, but then she said it again, perfectly, as if she'd been practising for months in secret. She wanted Erik to hear, but he had to come now, before it was too late. She leaned across Helene and knocked on the window, first with her knuckles, but when that didn't make enough noise she used the palms of her hands to thump the glass. She was so happy. Helene began to cry, frightened by the thudding, but Erik was still walking too slowly. Karin leaned forward between the front seats and honked the horn on the steering wheel. The sound made people turn round, and then it was Erik's turn to bang on the window. The car was locked; she pulled up the little knob and he yanked at the door. It sprang open as though there had been a vacuum.

'What's happened?' He was gasping for breath, leaning over into the back seat. 'What's happened?' he asked again. He examined Helene's face, stroking his fist over her sparse head of hair. 'Karin, you've got to answer me, what's happened?'

'She said Daddy.'

'What?'

'She said Daddy.'

He pulled back. 'You scared me to death.'

Helene had stopped crying. Erik crouched in front of the open car door, leaned across the child seat and stroked Karin on the arm and on the cheek. Something was stuck fast inside her.

'Hey, it's all right,' he said. He picked a long hair off her shoulder, continuing to rub her skin through her T-shirt. 'Karin. Look at me, please. You scared me, that's all. It's all right.'

When they had parked under the ferry deck, she turned to face him.

'What did you actually envisage?'

Helene is standing by the entrance down to the airport express train with one hand on her wheelie suitcase. She shakes a shiny watch out of her sleeve, looks down at it and glances around her. She looks beautiful in her grey coat, as sleek as a dolphin. Karin immediately feels big and awkward in her knitted dress. Her coat is full of fluff around the sleeves and along the sides, where her handbag rubs against her body.

'Nice bag,' says Helene when she sees her. 'Did you have to rush after all?'

'No, I had a glass of wine over there, and the waiter took ages when I wanted to pay.'

Helene nods and looks down at Karin's suitcase. It's big and soft with a red ribbon tied to the handle. When she was packing the night before, Karin couldn't think straight; she was tense and nervous, so she ended up taking far too much.

'Can you take that as cabin luggage?'

'I always use this, it's fine,' says Karin.

'Let's just hope the plane isn't full,' says Helene.

Karin examines her daughter's face and notices some dark spots in the corner of her mouth. 'You've got something there,' she says, pointing.

'Where?' says Helene. She drops the hair she was putting into a ponytail, touches her mouth and rubs at the wrong place at first. 'I had a brownie from Deli de Luca while I was waiting,' she says quickly. 'Shall we go?' She looks at the screens. 'There's one in three minutes. We'd better get it, or else we'll be late.'

Karin nods and starts walking towards the orange ticket machines on the wall, but Helene grabs her elbow.

'I've bought tickets,' she says, and lets go.

The plane is full. A flight attendant with a shaved head and powerful biceps helps Karin lift her suitcase into an overhead locker nearby, while men in suits with folded newspapers under their arms wait patiently for her to find her seat. Helene has already sat down; she puts a paperback and a bottle of sparkling water into the nylon pocket in front of her. Next to the window, there's a girl wearing a hoodie and big headphones. Karin sits down in the aisle seat and feels the warmth from Helene's body against her own. When they were buying coffee in one of the cafes at Oslo Airport, the woman behind the till overheard that they were going to London and asked if it was for Christmas shopping. Helene answered that they were on a 'mother and daughter weekend', which surprised Karin, even though it was technically correct. It came across as exaggerated and trivialized.

As the plane leaves the runway, Helene closes her eyes and grips the armrests so hard her tendons protrude under the skin on the back of her hands. There's something disturbing about observing her fear of flying close-up, maybe because her body is disclosing something she has never told anyone herself. It's only when the plane has risen above the clouds and the FASTEN

SEAT BELT signs are turned off that Helene opens her eyes again, as if nothing has happened. She takes a sip of water, bends down to get the bag she's shoved under the seat in front, and pulls out two glossy magazines she bought while they were waiting for boarding. The smell of deodorant hangs in the air, gritty and sour. A passenger on their way to the toilet treads on Karin's foot and both apologize.

During the flight they pass the magazines to each other. Karin knows Helene is friends with the editor of one of them, a beautiful woman in her mid-thirties who often speaks up in the media when the fashion industry is held to account. There's a black and white photo of her beside the editorial, where she writes about office Christmas parties. Karin quickly leafs through the magazine, fashion doesn't interest her, but she stops at an interview with the daughter of an ageing rock star, pictured in an industrial space that is almost stripped bare. The article describes how over the last two years the woman has got rid nearly all her possessions: clothes, furniture, cosmetics and so on. The goal, she says, is to be left with only her favourite, most essential and timeless things, produced in an ethically responsible way. It's all about rejecting consumer society and rediscovering life behind it.

Karin shows Helene the article. They haven't talked to each other for a while.

'It's supposed to be inspiring,' Helene says with a shrug.

A drinks trolley is pulled past on rickety wheels by the attendant who helped Karin with her suitcase. He looks like a football hooligan, but serves efficiently without any fuss. Helene orders white wine and pays for it. A couple of rows down there's a man crouching in the aisle, talking to the person in the seat nearest to him. He's holding a paper cup on the armrest, nodding regularly and meaningfully.

'Do you remember the flat you lived in right after you left Dad?' says Helene. She unscrews the lid of the little bottle of white wine and nods at the article still lying open on the tray table in front of Karin. 'It looked something like that, or actually it looked more like a hideout for human traffickers.'

It had been temporary accommodation, the only thing Karin could afford near Helene's nursery school. She rented a basement flat from a former colleague who lived on the floor above with her husband and two children. Before Karin moved in, the basement had housed an Eastern European nanny the children had outgrown.

'I have this memory of you boiling water for your coffee in a casserole dish, one of those huge ones you make stew in,' says Helene. She sips the wine and tops it up with the rest of the bottle.

'Did I? I can't remember doing that.'

Then she does recall a time when Helene came to stay and was sitting on the made-up sofa bed in her pyjamas. Karin was boiling up water to make hot chocolate with the powder she had bought, but the handles were unbearably hot when she held them, and the iron casserole was too heavy, so she dropped it and got boiling water all over her foot and parts of her calf. She must have screamed; the husband upstairs came down at least, maybe Helene had fetched him. He was the one who drove Karin to the casualty department while his wife, her former colleague, looked after Helene. Karin cried in the car, and in the waiting room her colleague's husband held his arm around her. When they came back, Karin with her foot bandaged, Helene was sitting in front of the TV with the other children. The sofa cushions were so big their feet hardly stuck over the edge, and their legs were covered with the same blanket. On the table there was strawberry squash, and on their laps they each had a bowl of oatmeal porridge. Their eyes sparkled at the video they were watching. When Karin told Helene it was time to go home, which meant walking down one flight of stairs, Helene wouldn't budge. She wanted to see the end of the film, and threw a tantrum.

'It was okay living there, wasn't it?' says Karin.

Helene rolls her eyes. 'You can just admit it was awful and laugh about it, you know?' Then she turns her attention back to her magazine.

'Anyway, I didn't live there very long,' says Karin.

They get to their hotel at 10.45 p.m. The man who welcomes them is young, with curly hair tied back in a ponytail. His cheeks are rough from acne scars and flushed, probably from a combination of shaving and shyness. After checking them in, he shows them up a narrow staircase with oat-yellow wall-to-wall carpeting that absorbs the sound of their steps, but not of the creaking planks. Both rooms are on the first floor, a couple of doors apart. They luckily have one each; Karin hasn't dared to ask. They agree to meet at reception in fifteen minutes to try and find somewhere still serving food. Karin unlocks the door. The room is small; it smells stale, and like industrial washing powder. At one end there's a queen-size bed and at the other a desk which, despite the size of the room, has a massive chair pushed against it. The back is one and a half metres high.

'I know – the chairs,' says Helene when they meet at reception. 'But it was the only hotel I could find round here that wasn't ridiculously expensive. It was a late booking.'

She has changed. Under her coat she's wearing a knee-length suede skirt and a white shirt. She studies the reception area coldly, moving her eyes from a stand with tourist brochures to a yellow sofa, where a young Asian couple are looking at something on a laptop. Then it's as if she thinks of something, or perhaps forgets where she is; her lips slip apart and Karin gets the feeling she is observing her at an unguarded moment. It's strange to have produced something so wonderful, Karin thinks, and is surprised by her own sentimentality. It sinks in that they have the whole weekend together, just the two of them. She wants to freeze this moment, stand another hour in the dingy reception looking at her daughter, but Helene suddenly seems impatient. 'Shall we go?' she says.

It has been raining. The air outside is mild, with wafts of cooking oil and rubbish. Helene walks on ahead, past Victorian houses with pillars and sash windows. Along Portobello Road they find a Vietnamese restaurant where they have a quick bite, then they go to a pub with its name written in gold letters on a green sign, and large wooden tables and patio heaters outside. Inside it's almost full, but they find a small table near the entrance. While Helene is at the bar, Karin looks around the place. In a booth nearby sit four young girls, maybe students; all are pretty, but one in particular is attracting attention, something her three friends seem to be used to. They have exaggerated facial expressions, but the prettiest one appears relaxed, nodding at what the others are saying. When she gets up from the table, her skirt sticks to her nylon tights and she pulls it loose with one hand.

'Hey.' Helene snaps her fingers in the space between them. There are two glasses of white wine on the table. 'You're staring.'

'Am I?' says Karin.

'What are you looking at?'

Karin shakes her head, smiling. The bartender comes over with a bowl of crisps they haven't ordered, but it looks like everyone gets one. Helene picks up a crisp from the bowl and places it in her mouth, then chews it so slowly it hardly makes a sound.

'Endre hasn't called,' she says. 'I don't really want him to call, but he promised he would after he'd put the kids to bed.'

She takes her phone out of her coat pocket, writes a message and puts it down on the table with the screen up. The background image shows Aldo and Lea with red cheeks, smiling. They look secure and well brought up. Helene and Endre are good parents; they care for their children with consideration and discipline, like a good team. Karin can't understand how they cope with the daily choreography behind hectic family life, the way two beings must work together to get a child ready to go out for a walk, for example. It seems like they are never in doubt about what the situation demands of them. She remembers a time she saw Helene stuff a dummy into Aldo's mouth on a packed bus. When he spat it out, she just stuffed it back in again. She kept pressing the dummy into his unwilling mouth while she talked unperturbed to Karin, as though she was convinced what she was doing was right. This had impressed Karin – where did she get that certitude from? – but at the same time there was something chilling about it. There was a hardness, with the same question hanging over it: Where did she get it from?

'Are the kids okay?' Karin asks.

'That's what I want to ask him,' says Helene. She presses the home button on her phone and the picture of the children lights up again, still without new messages in the foreground. 'He's not going to answer. He leaves his phone to charge in the kitchen when he goes to bed, it's something he's started doing recently. He says he doesn't want it in the bedroom because radiation is bad for the thyroid. It's really annoying. What if there's an emergency? He only thinks about himself.' She lifts another crisp from the bowl but lets it go, and brushes the salt off her fingers with a napkin.

The flow of words and the neurotic gestures stress Karin out, so she tries to do the same for Helene as she does for herself: focus on simple, concrete things. 'Thyroid?' she says. 'Is that the one behind the brain?'

'No, here,' says Helene. She points to the bottom of her throat. Karin finds herself mirroring the gesture; she pushes her index finger in carefully at the same point and immediately gets a choking sensation.

'And it gets damaged when you talk on your phone?'

'That's what Endre thinks. But this is all stuff he's read about or been told. Who knows what sources he uses.'

'Is it cancer?'

'What do you mean?'

'Can you get cancer, is that what's dangerous?'

'If you're so interested in this you should really ask Endre. I don't know. I hold the phone against my head all the time. I'm sure you get more ill from thinking so much about everything that might be dangerous. From a medical point of view, stress is the most dangerous thing there is.'

With impeccable timing, Karin takes a packet of cigarettes from her bag and asks if it's okay if she pops out for a minute. She stands under a heater, thinking about a meal she had at Helene and Endre's a year ago. They were eating sushi from a big black tray, and for want of a better topic of conversation Karin told them she was trying to give up smoking. It was only half the truth; she had started again the day before, after two jittery days without, but she wanted Helene's approval as they finished what had been a silent and awkward supper. Endre, who was busy peeling Aldo's sticky fingers off a phone, looked up from the end of the table. He asked her if she had read Allen Carr, which she hadn't, and then he went over to the bookcase, found a pink paperback and handed it to her across the table.

'It's a classic in this genre,' he said. 'I quit overnight.'

'I didn't know you used to smoke.' Karin looked at him, then at Helene, who was staring passively at Aldo. Lea was asleep upstairs.

'Not every day, but I was definitely a social smoker. I could easily smoke five in a row at parties. Do you remember, Helene?'

'Yes,' said Helene.

'I have an addictive personality,' he continued. 'Always have had. Two beers and I was obsessed' – he arched his eyebrows melodramatically – '*ob-sessed* with the thought of a cigarette. When Helene got pregnant I wanted to give up completely, so I did some research, came across this book and was convinced by the reviews on Amazon. Carr used to smoke a hundred a day, so you can just imagine.'

Karin sat with the book in front of her without opening it. There was low music coming from various black loudspeakers placed around the room, a strangely sensual tune controlled by Endre's phone. No, she just couldn't imagine. Instead, she thought about the cigarette breaks on the steps with Helene, trying to work out how many years had passed since then. Did Endre know Helene used to smoke too?

Endre lifted Aldo onto his lap and stroked his blonde curls. 'I noticed how much soy sauce you use,' he said to Karin. 'That's because your taste buds are ruined by smoking. That's what happens when you fill your body with poison every day. Your senses get dulled.'

Helene looked at him with a vague warning sign in her eyes, but she still didn't say anything.

'The amazing thing is that only eight hours after you've stubbed out your last cigarette, you're ninety-seven per cent nicotine free,' Endre continued. 'And after three days? A hundred per cent. *One hundred per cent.* They shouldn't really tell people that if the goal is to scare them off from starting.' He placed his hands playfully over Aldo's ears. 'He's just like me, he'll try anything.'

Aldo tried to wriggle away, to extract himself from the soundproofing grip. Endre laughed but let go in the end, holding his son round his middle instead, in a sort of cuddle.

'What day are you on?' he asked. 'As a non-smoker, I mean.'

Karin answered that she was only on day two, worried he could see she wasn't one hundred per cent. It was safest to put herself in the intermediate stage. She said she tried to go for walks or eat grapes if the urge to smoke became too overpowering, anything to keep the conversation going.

Endre gave an empathetic nod. 'Carr recommends you don't use substitutes like that, but you can read more about it yourself. Nicotine withdrawal is an extremely mild feeling. What's unpleasant – the only thing that's unpleasant, really – are the thought processes triggered by refusing yourself something you want. But the rewards are enormous.' Helene had got up to clear the table, and Endre was following her with his eyes. 'When you're ready to do it, it's easy.'

Karin stubs out her cigarette in the metal cylinder fixed to the pub wall and pushes the butt through the little grille. A young man from the group standing a few metres away turns round and looks at her. He smiles, he's maybe in his thirties, wearing a trench coat and a blue knitted hat with ear flaps. She considers having another smoke, but decides against it and goes back inside to Helene. There are two women talking intensely just inside the door; the one in a boob tube is hugging herself. Helene has bought two more glasses of wine and is on her phone.

'I guess it's something to do with his age,' Karin says when she has sat down. 'This stuff with Endre. He's nearly forty, isn't he?'

Helene shrugs. 'In the beginning I thought he'd been talked into joining an ecological sect, or at least I joked about it with my friends.'

'Maybe it's got something to do with conspiracy theories?' says Karin.

'What do you mean?'

'I've been reading about it, how the food industry and governments work together to poison people for profit.'

'That sounds very far-fetched,' says Helene. She rotates her glass and appears hypnotized by the wine sloshing about. 'He's always been preoccupied by his body, and I can sort of understand him. I remember how disgusting I felt during my pregnancies, and how much I exercised afterwards. I could sit with a pair of tweezers for hours, tweaking out the hair the wax strips had left behind. Now I've had it all removed by laser, I feel much better.'

Karin asks if Helene has had it all removed, which she has – 'everything from the neck down'.

'But for Endre it's so all-consuming,' she says. 'Sometimes I wonder if it's really just to do with his guilty conscience.'

'About what?'

The bartender comes and replaces the half-empty crisp bowl. Two men in suits have gone over to the table with the young girls. The prettiest girl is the only one who doesn't look sceptical; she's just indifferent, as though she understands she is the reason they have come over but at the same time it's up to her friends to turn them down. One of the men soon returns to his mates sitting at a table nearer the bar, but the other one takes a seat. He sits with half his bottom off the bench, supported by an outstretched leg, with a white circle of skin visible above his sock. The man looks drunk and uncomfortable. The beautiful girl stares down at her phone, while the others seem lost, sending each other frustrated, meaningful looks.

'I went with him to one of those meditation classes once,' says Helene.

They had sat on the floor and been asked to label inner observations, sift thoughts from feelings, and it was important that this happened continuously, as if one's inner life was passing by on a conveyor belt and should either have a blue or red lid.

'I couldn't separate them,' says Helene. 'It was like each feeling was a reaction to a thought, instead of the other way round. But it was the other way round that seemed to be the right answer.'

They walk in silence back to the hotel. The tarmac is shiny in the yellow glow of the street lights, and it's nearly 3 a.m. Even though they walk at the same pace, Helene is a few metres ahead. Her ponytail swings behind her with each movement, as if the present day is painting over an old, complex image. After she had learned how to walk, Helene refused to sit in her pram. If she was forced to, usually by Erik and often if they were late, she screamed non-stop until she was lifted out again, and at best would sit on his shoulders. When Karin was alone with her, there was never a problem. She liked to push the empty pram behind the trotting child, who never stopped unless she had something to say. Erik thought it was strange Helene didn't look behind her to check there was someone there. He would sometimes catch her, lift her up and throw her around so she laughed. Every time he did that, Karin felt a twinge of irritation. She felt he was intruding on Helene's bubble under the pretence of play. Personally, she preferred to let her walk alone by herself. It was like she was tied to her by an invisible rope, which tightened or loosened depending on the situation, and she thought that's why Helene didn't need to look behind her, because she felt the rope attached to her back somewhere. It was love the way she herself wished to experience it. She had been so proud.

Just before they go their separate ways in the narrow hotel corridor, Helene turns to face Karin. 'She's giving a lecture here on Sunday,' she says. 'I've bought tickets.'

'Who is?'

'The woman Endre's had an affair with.'

'She's here? In London?'

'Yes. She's going to talk at some kind of yoga festival, just nearby. I thought we could go.'

Karin can't decide whether she feels tricked, or if she's glad to have a plan to follow for their stay. 'Does Endre know she's here?' she says.

'If he does, he didn't dare say anything to me,' says Helene.

After they have said goodnight, Karin lies there in the hotel bed unable to fall asleep. A couple of times she dozes off but wakes up with her heart thumping, as though she has caught herself doing something irresponsible. She gets up and finds the key card with the password to the Wi-Fi network written on it in ballpoint pen. Then she grabs her phone from the bedside table, logs on to the internet and writes the address of Charlotte's blog. She scrolls down to the film she saw at home, from the Finnish meditation conference, and watches it again with what she imagines are Helene's eyes. In her head she rehearses things she can whisper during the lecture, and notices how her lips are moving. After the film, suggestions appear for other videos on a similar theme. Karin chooses one of them at random and lies watching a teenager with sparkling eyelids demonstrate how to do lymph drainage on your own body with 'easier movements than many people imagine'.

The next morning they go out to find somewhere to have breakfast. The Saturday market in Portobello Road is already open; tourists are chatting enthusiastically with stallholders and everyone is moving either too slowly or too fast, like extras in a film. Karin's hair is still wet from the shower, but the sun is hot, despite it being the middle of November. They stop at certain stalls but soon move on. Karin wonders if Helene has read Charlotte's blog; she wants to ask, though she can't bring herself to do so. Instead she comments on the surroundings in an artificially good mood that immediately makes her feel disheartened. There are two glossy dachshunds standing beside a bin, licking bits of icing from a muffin wrapper. It smells of mothballs and cooking fumes.

Helene finds what she thinks is a nice cafe on a corner. It's full, like everywhere else, but they manage to get a table by the window when a couple start to leave. The waiter, a young man with bleached hair and a ring in his nose, wipes over the table and leaves two menus, which turn out to have a Scandinavian theme. They order coffee, oatmeal porridge and toasted rye bread. It's Helene who in the end brings up the lecture, but without looking at Karin this time. It starts at eleven o'clock the next day, she says; they'll have plenty of time before their evening flight, she only wants to check it out.

'Is that why we're here?' says Karin.

'I just want to see her,' says Helene. 'What's so weird about that?'

'I didn't say it was weird.'

'Then we don't need to talk about it.'

The coffees arrive and Helene asks for some hot milk. She gets it served in a small ceramic jug, which she holds up in front of her admiringly. The waiter smiles when she tells him how much she likes it. It's made by a local potter, he says, and is for sale in a shop nearby. Helene listens attentively and thanks him profusely for the information. It was nothing, answers the waiter, and of course he's right. It annoys Karin to see how she puts on an act for strangers.

Helene tears open a pink paper sachet of artificial sweetener. She empties half of it into her cup and the rest into her porridge, stirring it in with the same spoon. They don't speak. While Helene is on her phone, Karin looks out of the window. A man in a suit and overcoat drags a dustbin onto the pavement to make room so he can reverse out a silver-grey Porsche.

'Anything special you'd like to do today?' says Helene. She has placed her napkin on top of what's left of the toast, but still keeps pulling off bits of bread with her fingers, putting them in her mouth with a faraway look on her face.

'Nothing specific,' says Karin.

Helene looks at her. 'What does "specific" mean?'

'I'll do whatever you want to do.'

Helene wants to 'hit the shops' because she so rarely has a chance to do so at home. They hail a taxi and drive in increasingly heavy traffic towards Oxford Street. The streets are decorated for Christmas with garlands and shiny baubles, but the trees in Hyde Park still have their leaves. In the central reservation by a pedestrian crossing, two women are hugging each other. Karin watches them while the taxi waits at a red light. They are both wearing turquoise uniforms under puffa jackets; one has her dark hair pinned up with a clasp, and it looks like she's the one being comforted. They have white slip-on shoes, and this makes Karin wonder if they're maids, nannies maybe? She has the feeling of having intruded on a story more dignified, more authentic than her own. The traffic light turns green and the taxi jerks forward. She turns in her seat so as not to lose sight of the embrace, but the women have already let go of each other.

The shop they arrive at is as big as a mall. Just inside the doors there are employees holding tablets, and a shiny series of escalators carry customers between the floors. They are assailed by voices and music from all sides; it's a nightmare. Wherever she looks, Karin sees girls and women hunting for something to buy. They pull clothes from racks as if they're collaborating on an urgent mission. Karin can't understand why Helene would want to come here, but she says nothing. They stop in front of the store guide, and a woman immediately comes over to them. She's young, slightly hunched over, wearing glittery silver leggings and a netting poncho over a black, tight-fitting top. On her head is a wide-brimmed hat. 'Ladies!' she says. 'Are you looking for anything in particular?'

Karin's instinct is to say no, but Helene answers the question as though it's been asked out of sincere curiosity. She says she's looking for 'something smart', a dress, a pair of trousers, and a jacket to go with them. The woman in the hat nods solemnly and seems to be thinking hard. Her hair falls over her shoulders in stiff waves. The best thing, she says, and definitely the most efficient, would be to use one of the store's personal shoppers. The service costs fifty pounds an hour, but is free if you end up buying more than three items of clothing. Fruit juice, tea and coffee are included in the price.

'And then you don't have to queue up for the fitting rooms, which' – she lowers her voice as if they're part of a conspiracy – 'can be hell, to be honest.'

Helene glances at Karin. 'That sounds all right, doesn't it?'

Karin pictures herself sitting in a comfortable chair, away from the crowds and the music. Personally, she buys most of her clothes and shoes online; she can't bear the thought of being surrounded by people right when she desires an item enough to actually pay for it. Maybe it's to do with the customers in the jewellery shop, grown-up people who ask to have a display case unlocked, then hold the piece of jewellery against their skin with a look of restrained greed in their eyes while she stands silently next to them, watching. She never gets used to it. However civilized the situation appears, she thinks of them as children. A lot of them try to rise above the loss of authority by treating her like a servant, formulating their questions like orders, but the truth is that they ask and she consents. They covet and she doesn't care.

'Sounds good,' says Karin.

'Great,' says the woman in the hat. She consults her tablet and asks them to wait at the bottom of the escalator on the floor below. 'Rosie will meet you there,' she says. 'I think she's wearing leather trousers.'

'They're not leather,' Rosie laughs when Helene mentions what the woman in the hat has said. 'They're synthetic. I sweat like a pig each time I wear them.'

Now she has diverted attention to her thighs and body, Karin sees that she's quite plump but also well dressed; anything else would perhaps be unacceptable. Her tight curls have a wet texture and jump off her shoulders every time she laughs, which she does constantly.

She has taken them into a private room as big as the shop Karin works in. Again the floor is covered in wall-to-wall carpeting, this time low pile and creamy-white. There are two fitting rooms with pink velvet curtains that match the sofa they're sitting on. On the low table in front of them there are magazines spread out like a fan. Rosie is sitting with a tablet on her lap and her legs crossed, her trousers creaking like wet oilskins. Her face expresses a childlike gravity when she explains her 'philosophy'. She works 'one layer at a time, like a bricklayer', she says, and prefers simple styles which accentuate the customer's qualities without screaming for attention – 'Unless that's what the customer wants,' she adds quickly, clapping her hands. 'What are you looking for today, Helene?'

Helene explains again, like she did to the woman in the hat, but more precisely this time. Her voice is hesitant, as if she's finding and rejecting words while she talks. She looks for pictures on her phone, which Rosie studies carefully while taking notes. Karin is impressed by how seriously they take their roles, how supportive they are of each other's performance. After taking their juice orders and Helene's bust, waist and hip measurements, Rosie disappears to dig out what she calls 'candidates for the first round'.

'Do you want to see?' says Helene after she has gone.

'See what?'

'What I'm looking for.'

Helene moves closer to Karin on the sofa. She finds the pictures on her phone again, pretty women in pretty clothes against neutral backgrounds. She holds the screen low down in front of Karin, who nods approvingly. They soon come to photos of the children, of Aldo and Lea. In one of them they're sitting on Endre's parents' laps, engrossed by something going on in front of them; in another they're standing side by side on the decking in the garden, Lea with a fat tummy and tangled hair. Then they're suddenly in Italy, with their backs to the waves and excited faces, playing with beach toys, white and grainy from sun lotion and sand. There's one of Aldo, ill with fever, his swollen face partly buried under a duvet with jungle animals on the cover, and selfies of Helene and Endre smiling tensely at the camera. Endre is driving a jet ski, reading to Lea, red-eyed and drinking white wine at a beach club. Helene says nothing. She no longer holds up the phone, at least not in the same way as before, but slightly lifts her finger from the screen for each photo before swiping further. When she comes to pictures of the house, of the kitchen being renovated, ripped apart and laid bare, she closes the app and puts the phone back in her handbag.

An athletic-looking man in yellow trousers comes in with the juice they have ordered, two see-through plastic cups of green liquid that looks like it's been drained from an abandoned aquarium. Helene stands up to take them.

'Who's looking after you today?' he asks before leaving.

'Rosie,' says Helene.

'You're in luck there,' he says. 'She's an angel.'

Soon after, Rosie comes in backwards through the door, pulling a rack of muted fabrics arranged over a couple of dozen coat hangers. She jerks it to get the wheels over the threshold. 'Shall we start with the dresses?' she says to Helene. 'Or are you the type who would rather get the trousers out of the way first?'

'Dresses are fine,' says Helene, getting up.

Rosie lifts a sand-coloured dress with long sleeves from the rack and hangs it up on a hook in the fitting room. Helene follows her. They exchange a few words about the dress's misleading shape on the hanger, before Rosie pulls the pink curtain closed with a firm hand, as though she's the assistant in a magic show and Helene a member of the audience who has volunteered to disappear.

For a while Karin doesn't hear anything other than the rustling of clothes. She tears the paper off a straw and pokes it down into the juice through a hole in the arched plastic lid. It tastes sour and bitter.

Rosie moves the hangers around on the rack, shoving assortments of clothes away from each other without hesitation. 'How's the juice?' she asks. 'My favourite's the one with beetroot and apple. If only I could just stick to that, but I've always got to have something sweet to go with it, a muffin or choco-late to balance the bitter taste, otherwise I get a headache.'

The ice cubes have started to melt and the plastic cup sweats against the inside of her hand. Karin puts it down on the low table and dries her hands on her trousers with splayed fingers, continuing to stroke them up and down to calm herself. She suddenly thinks about Torstein, about the soft dips in his lower back where she cuddled up to him in the dark.

'How's it going in there, Helene?' says Rosie. 'Do you need help with the zip?'

Helene mumbles something or other. Rosie looks at Karin, as if to ask for help translating, then shrugs and walks over to the sofa. Her high heels dig down into the carpet, but she walks upright and elegantly with her weight on the balls of her feet. She sits down on the arm of the sofa, bouncing one foot in the air in front of her.

'Now you must be honest and say what you think, okay?'

Karin nods, while realizing she won't be able to play the role to Rosie's satisfaction. 'But I think my daughter knows best,' she says, to avert disappointment.

'Your daughter?' Rosie raises her eyebrows and opens her mouth in exaggerated amazement. 'But you're so young! I thought you were colleagues.'

The curtain rings scrape against the rail and Helene treads barefoot out of the fitting room. Her body is long and slim; she's always been sporty. If followed with a pencil, the outline of Helene's body is not unlike Karin's.

Rosie gets up and walks towards Helene, but stops, drawing a cross in the air with her index finger. 'Now I can see it,' she says. 'Same nose and lips.'

Helene glances at Karin before concentrating on Rosie again, who is kneeling to help her into a pair of high-heeled shoes. Helene has to support herself against Rosie's shoulder with one hand when she steps into the other shoe. Her toenails are glossy burgundy. Then Rosie stands up straight and slides a finger under the modest neckline of the dress to loosen a few folds in the material. It's an intimate gesture, Karin thinks, but the two other women seem unfazed by it. Rosie studies Helene with an expert's confident scepticism, takes off two plastic clips she has had fastened to the edge of her shirt and uses them to gather some of the fabric in the back of the dress. It sits better straight away.

'That's better, isn't it?' says Rosie. 'We've got an in-house tailor who can fix that sort of thing in less than a day.'

Helene turns round and looks at herself uncertainly in the mirror. She fetches her phone from the fitting room and asks Karin to take a picture. Karin has to step back a bit and crouch down in order to get in the whole of Helene, who is posing slightly. Afterwards it looks like Helene sends the picture to someone.

'Wait there, let's try it with some jackets,' says Rosie.

She goes over to the rack, clutches a whole assortment of clothes, lifts them with her knees so the hooks of the hangers come off the rail, then drapes them over the arm of the sofa. With nimble fingers she helps Helene into a velvet jacket, quickly assesses it and repeats the process with two others, first a tweed jacket then a shiny blazer. Rosie adjusts the fit of the last one by pushing her hand under the back of the jacket.

'You must have been young,' she says, meeting Karin's eye over Helene's shoulder. 'When you became a mother, I mean.'

'I don't know. Twenty.'

'About the same as me,' says Rosie. 'I was twenty-one. He's four now.'

'Do you live in town?' asks Helene.

'Liam lives with my mum in Brent, not too far away. I live there too, but when I work here and if I have early lectures, I stay at my boyfriend's.'

She's in her third year of fashion design, she tells them. She really wants to go on and do a master's, but she's not sure she can afford it. Then she would need another job, as well as this one. She feels that she sees too little of Liam as it is.

'My dad called me a fool when I started studying fashion, with Liam at home and everything, and I know it's a difficult business, but it's my passion. I said to him: "You don't choose your dreams." Do you like the shoes?' Rosie nods at the pair Helene has on. They're reddish brown with pointed toes.

'The colour's lovely,' says Helene.

'I've got another pair over here.'

These ones are green with leather straps that fasten round the ankles. Rosie kneels again and fiddles with the buckles. Helene asks whether her father has come to terms with her career choice now.

'He's from Algeria,' she says, as if that's all the answer she needs.

While Helene changes, Rosie talks about her family. Her father met her mother in Paris, where she went to learn French. After a year they moved to England, got married and had children. Soon after Rosie was born, he returned to his religion, which he had rejected as a teenager.

'He started going to the mosque again,' says Rosie.

Helene asks if anything particular happened to trigger this.

'I think having children made him feel the need for something bigger, a meaningful system to raise us in,' says Rosie.

Her parents are still married, but they don't live together any more, not since Rosie got pregnant five years ago. Now her father works as a security guard for a stockbroking firm in the City and she doesn't have much contact with him.

'My mum calls him the ayatollah. "Have you heard from the ayatollah?" she asks, but if I talk to him he just goes on about wanting to go home – he hates this country, the politicians, the people, the weather. And he still has family in Algeria, but what would he do there? He hasn't lived there for thirty years. He's getting on a bit.' She rocks back and forth on one heel. 'Everyone always asks me how they could have stayed together so long, but my mum needed his salary to live where we did. She sacrificed herself for us.'

Helene has put on a pair of shiny trousers and an olive-coloured blouse. She's listening with her head cocked, and looks like a dancer learning her steps.

'Even when I made the same mistake as her and fell in love with the wrong guy, she was there for me,' Rosie continues. 'Saved me, really. Well, Liam's the best thing that's ever happened to me, of course. As soon as I've finished uni and started my own collection, we're going to find a flat together, me and my boyfriend, and Liam will have his own bedroom.'

Helene says it sounds great, and asks what her boyfriend does.

'He's a chef,' says Rosie. 'And he's brilliant with Liam. Makes him fried eggs that look like pirates, don't ask me how. Liam goes on about it every morning, but my mum has no idea how to make them.'

She laughs again. Then she goes into the fitting room and hangs up a skirt and a sweater, before ordering Helene in and pulling the curtain across. She sits on the edge of the sofa next to Karin.

'Do you live in the same town as Helene?' she says.

Karin nods.

'It must be nice to have your grandchildren nearby,' says Rosie. 'And great for Helene, at least. I don't know what I would have done without my mum.'

Karin can see Helene's bare feet under the curtain. They don't move. Rosie reaches behind her for the water dispenser, pulls a plastic cup out of the transparent tube and fills it up. The container bubbles. She drinks it all and fills the cup again. Her personality expands into the room, filling every corner it finds with light. There's something domineering about it, like in the fable where the sun shows its strength by shining on the man until he has no other choice but to get undressed.

'I had to become a mother myself before I understood it, how much you're willing to give up,' says Rosie. 'Liam is my whole world, right? My mum always says you should form a meaningful system with the people you love. I try to live by that.'

Helene finally comes out of the fitting room. She's wearing a patterned skirt and a light, long-sleeved top. Her cheeks are glowing. 'What do you think?' she says.

'You look beautiful,' says Karin. She feels a pressure in her chest; she suddenly wonders who took Helene to look at wedding dresses, or if she sorted it out by herself, but Helene isn't looking at Karin, she's looking at Rosie. The question was to her.

It's almost two when they leave the shop. The sky is heavy with grey clouds. Both of them feel drowsy after spending so long in that artificially heated room. Helene carries a big, stiff carrier bag in one hand that knocks against her ankles as she walks. The sand-coloured dress has been sent to the tailor and will be ready the next day. Before they left, Rosie hugged them both. Karin got her hair in her face. 'I hope you'll be happy with everything,' said Rosie.

Helene walks ahead to a little restaurant with green plants and mirrors on the walls. They're given the Wi-Fi password by the waiter and they both sit there on their phones. Helene orders a 'warm winter salad', but when the food arrives, she pushes the root vegetables around the plate sceptically. She insists that it tastes odd, but when the waiter asks how it is, she smiles and answers, 'Everything's great, thanks.'

While they sit with their coffees, Karin gets a message from Torstein. *Ms Bardot is keeping a low profile*, it starts. *How about a beer and maybe a bite to eat as well?* She replies that she's in London. *Hey, hey, have fun*, he writes. A few minutes later it beeps again. *What about next week? Then you can tell me all about Big Ben.* The vague sexual innuendo makes her laugh.

Helene looks up from her phone in surprise. 'What are you laughing at?'

'Only something on the internet.'

Helene smiles. 'Let's see.'

'No, it wasn't that funny.'

'It obviously was.' She glances curiously at Karin's phone, but Karin puts it back in her bag. Helene rolls her eyes. 'I've been mailing with some of my friends from my exchange year who live here,' she says. 'I might see them tonight. About eight or nine. Would you like to come?'

'Eight or nine people?'

'O'clock.'

'Do you want me to come?'

'I just asked you.'

'But aren't they all your age?'

'That doesn't matter. The question is do you want to.'

It's impossible to know what Helene hopes she will answer, but Karin would actually like to see her in the company of old friends. She never visited Helene during the year she spent at the University of Leicester, but they stayed in touch by phone and Karin had the impression she was enjoying herself. She returned home with a slightly naive political commitment and a skinny body Karin assumed was modern. 'Sure,' she says.

A woman at the table next to them bursts into loud, forced laughter. The man she's sitting with looks around the room with an apologetic yet proud smile. He probably thinks her laugh is genuine.

'Fine,' says Helene. 'Then I'll tell them we're both coming.' She checks her watch and indicates to the waiter that they would like the bill.

'But won't they think it's strange that I'm there?'

It's the third time Karin has asked. They have had a shower and changed, and now they're standing at reception. Helene's eyes keep darting around the room as though she's keeping tabs on an insect. 'I've no idea,' she says. 'It doesn't matter. Ed says he's looking forward to meeting you.'

'Who's Ed?'

'One of the friends we're going to see,' says Helene.

Karin has put her hair up, and a pair of long, clear crystal earrings knock coldly against her neck each time she moves her head. It took her a long time to put on her make-up; she removed it all twice and began again. Now her eyes feel sore and dry, but her eyeliner is even. Helene's wearing the skirt and green shoes she bought earlier. She looks overdressed, Karin thinks, but it suits her. It reminds Karin of when Helene was a teenager.

In the taxi Helene sits with a map open on her phone, following the blue dot through the streets and staring outside. The pub they have arranged to meet at turns out to be a restaurant, with a maze of dimly lit lounges in burnt colours. There are large mirrors and framed pictures in different sizes hanging on the walls, with a stuffed animal head here and there. They find Helene's friends at a table by the wall in the biggest room, where the bar is. One of them, the one called Ed, explains that it's fine just to have a drink, but that they plan to have something to eat too. There are four of them, two men in addition to Ed and a woman who looks younger. Her nipples are showing through her white top, which has a red rose embroidered approximately where the heart is. She has tied back her long fair hair with a black bow. She's called Hailey and is the girlfriend of one of the men, a guy in a suit. It's only later, when they have ordered beer and a bottle of red wine plus some dishes to share, that Karin gets a chance to study the men. Ed is tall, with a few centimetres of dark hair, and is dressed in a coarse, beige shirt and black jeans. He has a big mouth and a gold ring in one of his ears. The one in the suit is called Jack and is handsome in a rather old-fashioned way: blue flashing eyes, a triangular nose and heavy eyebrows. The last one, a short guy with glasses and wavy chestnut hair, is called Anthony, but is known as Ant, he says. She has shaken everyone's hand, Helene got hugs. Their knees knocked against the underside of the table when they half stood up and reached towards her.

'What have you done today?' asks Jack.

'Just wandered around and had lunch,' says Helene.

'Did you go to the exhibition I told you about?' says Ed.

Helene shakes her head.

'Which one?' asks Hailey.

'Egon Schiele at Somerset House,' says Ed.

When she was younger, Karin would often tell men she wanted to sleep with that she loved Egon Schiele. It had the greatest effect if they didn't know who he was and she could describe the pictures she liked best: She's lying on her stomach with her dress pulled up around her waist…

A tall woman with red lips and short curls puts the first dishes on the table. They look greasy and oily. No meat. Jack and Hailey are vegetarians, they explain, and Ant tries to avoid meat but eats it if that's what is served. He calls himself a flexitarian. 'Vegetarianism for introverts,' says Ed.

The waiter takes new orders. Hailey wants some white wine; Jack says there's already red wine on the table.

'Red wine makes me tired,' she says.

The bowls are passed round and the food spread onto dark plates. In the bar area there are guests sitting with their jackets on their laps waiting for tables. Two men have given up and are eating at the bar. They hang over their plates, chatting loudly. Outside, visible through the large windows, there's a group of people smoking. A woman in a leather jacket shows off with a dance to keep warm, or to charm the man she's with.

After half an hour, no one has asked anyone about their current circumstances. In the end, Karin asks what they all do. They take it in turns to answer dutifully and she feels stupid to have asked, or just feels old. The men have all studied political science, that's how they know each other. Ed has just moved home after some years at Berkeley, where he took a master's degree, and now works for a non-profit organization which campaigns to end London's investments in fossil fuels. Jack is a lawyer in a medium-sized company that specializes in corporate law, and hopes to become a partner. Ant finished his studies and ended up in an administrative post at the National Portrait Gallery, rather by chance. He enjoys it, at least for the time being.

'I run my own company,' says Hailey. 'I make jewellery.'

She puts down her knife and fork and holds up both hands. Her nails are bright orange, and on one hand she has three simple gold rings. On the other she has a ring with a pink stone, which she says is rose quartz.

'It has healing qualities,' she says, caressing the stone with the index finger of her other hand. 'It balances and soothes your feelings.'

'She's a trained goldsmith,' says Jack, stroking her back. 'A creative genius.'

Hailey smiles. Karin feels her chest tighten as if she's been caught lying, even though she hasn't lied yet.

'I started off studying art, but I dropped out,' says Hailey. 'It wasn't practical enough, and I like working with things that are a part of people's everyday lives. It's beautiful for me to think of one of my rings submerged in dirty washing-up water, or stroking a warm horse. A friend of mine does showjumping,' she explains. 'For her birthday I made her a ring with a blood-stone – that's what the Greeks called it – which is supposed to strengthen your body and increase your stamina.'

Jack says something Karin doesn't quite hear, and the men laugh.

'I also think like an entrepreneur,' says Hailey. 'I like going to meetings and making deals. There's already three shops in London selling my collection.' It's the most she has said since they sat down.

'Karin works at a jeweller's,' says Helene.

'Who?' says Hailey.

'My mum,' says Helene, nodding at Karin. 'She works in a jewellery shop back in Oslo.'

'Really?' says Hailey. 'Maybe you could sell my collection. It'd be cool to get established in Norway. I love Scandinavian design.'

Karin tries to smile. It goes quiet again.

'Is there any more red wine?' says Ed.

Helene lifts the empty bottle. They order another one. When Karin stands up to have a cigarette, Jack and Ant join her outside. She tries her best to think of good, interesting questions but ends up asking how they got to know Helene. Jack says they noticed her at lectures, sitting alone. She was in the same seminar group as Jack and he introduced her to the others. She was like an exotic bird, he says, and they were all in love with her. 'That's why we hate Ed.'

They look at Karin.

'It was a joke,' says Ant, when she doesn't laugh.

When they come back to the table, Helene is sitting with her arms crossed, smiling at Ed. She strokes her elbow while she listens to what he says. Hailey has moved to Karin's chair, to be nearer the others, but gets up when she sees them coming.

'You can just sit there,' says Karin.

'No, don't be silly, have your place back,' says Hailey, and returns to the seat next to Jack, who puts his arm around her.

Karin has a feeling they're all putting up with her, not just Helene. She feels she's being badly treated, without knowing exactly why. All the same, she leans back in her chair, so no one can claim she's in the way. She tries to express detached amusement while the conversation moves round the table.

'There's a view of a fjord from your office?' Ed says to Helene, his eyes wide open. 'London offices either have a view of other London offices, or they cast shadows over the poor areas, usually both in fact.' He points at a sleek colossus on the other side of the street that looms over the low brick buildings like a dystopian tower. It's new, he says, erected in the rubble of a block of council flats. A few years ago they discovered a construction fault, something to do with the pipes, but instead of fixing it the local authority threw out the residents and sold the site to a private property developer. The luxury apartments that were built are now owned by Russian oligarchs and Saudi Arabian princes, who only spend a couple of weeks there a year. 'Just look,' says Ed. 'All the windows are dark, day and night.'

'What happened to the people who used to live there, in the old building?' says Helene.

Ed plunges a piece of bread into the asparagus dip, lifts it up high so the threads of gratinéed cheese fall off, and chews while he talks. 'London is corrupt from top to bottom. The government runs this town like the mafia.'

'Don't your parents own six flats in the centre?' says Jack.

Ed's jaw twitches. 'They're a part of the problem, I've always said so. And you are too, you bastard.'

Jack holds up his hands, laughing. 'Always said so,' he says. He cuts a leaf of chicory in two and puts one half in his mouth with his fork. 'But I'm still in touch with reality,' he continues. 'Being opposed to the basis of our entire economic system is just being deliberately ignorant, which I despise.'

His broad chest puffs up under his shirt when he leans back, revealing the outline of a string vest. He's also from London, he tells Karin, but from a different part of town, quite far south. His mother worked in a company canteen and raised him and his two siblings by herself. From the outside the life he lives today isn't so different from Ed's, he says.

'The difference is that I have worked for this lifestyle, and I'm up to my ears in debt, while you' – he looks at Ed, who's leaning back in his chair, pensively chewing the inside of his cheeks – 'with a father who went to Eton with half the government you're so critical of, you like to hide that you're rich. The result is a superficial levelling which covers over the fundamental injustice.' He starts to raise his wine glass to his mouth, but stops halfway. 'In fact, I'd say the best way to show solidarity is to be brutally honest with yourself about all the opportunities your background's given you, the circles you've been included in, and not least what you've got away with. I should know, I'm a lawyer.'

'I bet you've got away with a lot yourself,' says Helene.

'Of course,' says Jack, smiling. 'Brutal soul-searching is required of everyone.'

Helene snorts, a sound Karin has heard her make many times, though never at anyone but herself. 'You say that so complacently,' says Helene. 'But the problem is most people who do this brutal soul-searching don't see the whole picture. It's called a blind spot for a reason.' She holds up her right hand to show her wedding ring. 'I should know, I'm married.'

Ed glances at her.

'What do you mean?' asks Karin. Something in the tone of Helene's voice has made her curious.

'Just that you can never examine your faults from the right angle, at least not the important ones, because you are who you are. You're stuck with yourself as your starting point.'

'So you see no reason to be honest with yourself?' says Karin. 'I think that's strange.'

Helene stares back with an unreadable look in her eyes, then turns her attention to Jack. 'If you're lucky it leads to a glimmer of self-knowledge, but for what exactly? To become a better person? I don't think so.'

Helene reaches for the bottle of wine, fills up her glass, then Jack's, without meeting Karin's eye. Karin realizes she's being punished. By speaking up she tried to secure her place around the table, but Helene's reaction leaves her to understand that she is now on her own. She looks at Ant, who hasn't said anything for a while, and does her best to sound unconcerned. 'What about you, where are you from?'

The sound of his voice is a relief. He grew up in Oldham, he says, a small town outside Manchester, but his parents moved to Wales a few years ago, to the village his mother is from, near a bay. He has recently been thinking about moving there himself; he's tired of London. The town he dreamed about as a teenager doesn't exist any more, he says.

'If you close your eyes,' says Ed, 'you can almost hear the sound of Russian caviar against porcelain veneers.'

A waiter piles all their plates along his arm, creeping silently and seriously between them. Karin watches how his hips twist and turn towards the table each time he reaches across for empty bowls.

'I know someone who got ill from it, from living here,' says Hailey. 'Everything made him sick: washing powder, radiation, ink, radio waves. Now he's moved to the Scottish Highlands, where someone's started a campsite for people with environmental sensitivities.'

Karin tries to catch Helene's eye, but she's staring stiffly at Hailey while she fiddles with her necklace.

'They're cleansed of all toxins, as far as possible. And then it's far enough away from other people for him to manage, just about.'

'That doesn't make sense,' says Helene.

Hailey nods. 'I can't even visit him. Even the people living there can't visit each other. They all have different tolerance levels, and no one dares risk something that might harm them.'

'In a word,' says Jack, 'nutters.'

Karin searches for her packet of cigarettes in her coat pocket.

'I think it's pretty radical, personally,' says Hailey. 'Just think how demanding it must be.' She has finished her drink and says she knows of a club nearby where a friend of hers is playing. Her lips glisten with white wine and fruit juice, highlighting blonde hairs that curve down from her Cupid's bow to the corners of her mouth. 'Shall we go?'

Both Ed and Jack indicate that they want the bill.

The nightclub is in a basement. On their way down narrow concrete steps, they pass a cloakroom where a dark-haired woman in a tight denim waistcoat stares blankly at them. The first room they come to resembles a big cave. Narrow passages lead to other rooms, separated by transparent plastic curtains. It's almost one in the morning. Hailey goes off to find her friend. The music is incredibly loud, but in the dug-out courtyard at the back the sound is reduced to a heavy, rhythmic vibration. Round about there are patio heaters and large wooden tables, and paper lanterns printed with Chinese signs hanging on strings from the roof. They find a table, and Ed goes over to the bar with Helene. Ant glances over his shoulder at a group of young women in leather jackets huddled together round a table. Their false eyelashes make their faces look sleepy. He turns back and pulls his hood over his head. Karin tries to catch his eye; her tongue feels big and warm in her mouth, but he doesn't look at her. Ed comes back carrying a tray of beers, shot glasses and lime quarters on a napkin. Helene holds the door open for him. 'You drink tequila?' he says to Karin with a smile.

They all raise their glasses together, down them in one and bite on the limes. Jack reaches for the last glass, meant for Hailey, and knocks that back too. Then he gets up and disappears towards the bar. Through one of the windows Karin can see him make his way towards Hailey, who's standing on tiptoe next to her friend, with a hand cupped round his ear. Someone nudges Karin. Ed is holding out a beer for her. 'Sorry,' she says and takes it.

He raises his glass and wants to propose a toast, to Helene. 'It's good to see you,' he says. 'And of course to meet your mother. Here's to you both!'

Karin lights a cigarette and offers the packet to Ant. He shakes his head and takes out his own pouch of loose tobacco. With the white filter between his lips, he arranges the tobacco in the rolling paper. Karin follows his movements closely. His nails are dirty, dark strips under the white tips. She tries to lose herself in these observations. She knows that when she looks up, her presence will again feel like the most obtrusive one around the table. Ed wants to know what Helene's husband is called. He tries to pronounce it and fails. It sounds like *entrée*.

'It's tricky,' says Helene, and no one asks what she's referring to.

Bodies brush past and towards each other, leaving and returning to tables. They talk about China, polarization and terrorism, forming long chain arguments beginning with 'I feel'. Ed and Helene disappear and come back with more drinks. Karin feels like a voyeur, someone who doesn't belong there, but she also feels that the others have made her feel this way. She gets up to go to the toilet. The place has begun to fill up. She locks the cubicle door, pulls out her phone and calls Torstein. He answers straight away, but then asks what time it is and she realizes she has woken him. 'Sorry, we can talk another time,' she says.

'No, no.'

She hears him scrabbling about and pictures him propping himself up and turning on the light by the bed.

'Where are you?' he says.

She hesitates at first, then she tells him about the evening, the dinner with Helene's friends, the conversations and the club she's at. She tries to make it funny by including as many details as possible, smiling to herself as she talks. He remains quiet at the other end.

'Sorry,' he says after a few seconds. 'I'm only half awake. I must have been sound asleep.'

She feels foolish. She apologizes for calling so late, blaming the tequila.

'I'm glad you rang,' he says.

'Forget it,' she says, and hangs up.

She stands at the bar, trying to attract the bartender's attention. A pale-looking boy on her right asks for three shots, knocks one back and takes the other two over to a girl who's waiting in the blue light of her phone. The bartender turns to another customer.

'Hey, there you are.' It's Helene. 'You disappeared. Are you okay?' She smiles, seems genuinely interested in the answer, and Karin can't help picturing the scene that possibly took place at the table outside: Helene dropping out of the conversation, looking around, asking the others 'Where's Karin?' or even 'Where's my mum?', making the bond visible for everyone.

Helene lays her hand on Karin's back. 'Gin and tonic?' she says.

Karin laughs with relief. There and then it feels like the nicest thing Helene has ever said to her. 'Yes please, I'd love one.'

Helene gets the bartender's attention immediately. When the glasses come, she takes the straw out of hers and puts it down on the bar. 'Do you like Ed?' she says.

'He certainly seems to like you,' says Karin.

Helene laughs. Her hair has lost the volume it had earlier and lies flat against her head, but her face is warm and carefree. 'Yeah, I know,' she says. It looks like she's about to say more, her eyes are sparkling, but then she seems to get a grip on herself and withdraws behind a different, more diffuse facade. 'It's a bit awkward.'

They go back to their table. Hailey's on her phone, looking like a cuddly toy in her blue fake fur. Ant is fiddling with a lighter, and Ed and Jack are having yet another heated discussion.

'You can't seriously mean that,' says Ed. He stares at Jack. 'It's depressing coming from a lawyer like you.'

'I understand why the law must operate within clear boundaries, it's obvious. I'm just saying it must be possible to have more nuanced conversations about the subject,' says Jack. 'In reality, boundaries are never clear-cut. It's ridiculously naive to believe anything else.'

'The problem is that these conversations help to create a culture,' says Ed. 'That's precisely why it's so important to show exactly where you stand. And if you think consent is naive, then—'

Hailey says something about women being physically vulnerable by nature, and that it's precisely this vulnerability men don't understand, can't understand. Jack grabs her ponytail and pulls it back, asking what it is he doesn't understand. He's smiling, clearly joking, but Hailey doesn't laugh and asks him to let go. Instead, he pulls her head back even more. The tendons in her neck tighten when she tries to force herself up. Jack asks again what it is he doesn't understand.

'Let go,' says Hailey.

Then he lets go, and Hailey's head bobs up. She reaches for the black bow, which has slipped off in the struggle. Jack laughs, trying to pull her body close to his; he wants to kiss her, but she shakes him off, gets up and leaves. 'What happened?' asks Jack, confused. 'It didn't hurt, I was only kidding. It was a joke.'

When no one answers, he puts his head in his hands, pressing his palms hard against his temples. He repeats that it didn't hurt. Ed says it's okay, Hailey was probably just taken by surprise. When she returns to the table, she has tied back her hair again and is holding a plastic cup with clear liquid in it. Jack stares sadly into his beer. Ed and Helene continue a discussion about Norway versus Britain. Hailey sits back down beside Jack, lowers her head onto the table to get eye contact and whispers it's okay, but he doesn't budge.

'I don't understand,' he says.

—

Outside, the air is still mild and the pavement is packed. Ed wants to go to another bar, Hailey wants wine gums. Now she's on her feet, Karin notices how drunk she is; a heavy nausea sways in her stomach. She tries to find Helene, but she's already on her way down the road with Ed. Karin goes with Jack and Hailey towards a corner shop. When she looks around for a taxi, none of the cabs driving past have their lights on. She asks if there's a taxi rank nearby, but Hailey insists that she must come with them. 'Just one drink,' she says. 'I don't think Helene realized you were going to leave, so she'll be disappointed if you've suddenly gone.'

The yellow glow from street lights merges with the white from all-night convenience stores and the neon from clubs. Together they push past two red-faced men with dripping food in white paper wrappers, into the corner shop that obviously sells alcohol without a licence. A young South Asian boy runs back and forth between the shop and the stockroom, delivering clinking bags with a downcast look in his eyes. Karin asks for a packet of cigarettes. Jack waits outside, squinting at his phone. Hailey chews her way through a tube of red wine gums. A gang of boys in shiny bomber jackets go past, see Karin tearing the plastic off her cigarette packet and ask if they can bum one. She holds out the packet towards them and all four help themselves. The tallest one asks if she has a light, but when she holds it up for him he leans towards her with the cigarette in his mouth. He smells strongly of sweat. She takes a step back and his friends begin to laugh. Jack comes over and asks if everything's okay. The boy who has asked for a light says something Karin doesn't hear; he has a thick accent, made even more incoherent by alcohol. It takes a moment for Jack to understand the insult. He gets worked up, and Hailey has to drag him down the road in the other direction. The boys call after him, laughing hysterically.

One of them pulls up his T-shirt, revealing a hideous tattoo that covers the entire left side of his chest.

Outside the bar Ant is having a smoke, with a long-suffering expression on his face. Jack immediately starts telling him about the gang of boys, what they said, how he should have 'smashed the little cunts to bits'. Karin goes inside. It's dark and poky, with heavy wooden booths. The bartender is shaking a silver cylinder with vigorous jerks of the elbow. In one of the booths Ed and Helene sit facing each other, their heads close together. They resemble two swans in a kitsch painting, with eyes like black bullets. Someone starts singing along to a Rolling Stones tune without knowing the words, and the bartender rattles the cocktail shaker over the song like a percussion instrument. Karin moves closer. She can suddenly clearly visualize who Helene was when she came back from England, so hollow-faced and serious, but also arrogant, convinced she was pursuing a greater truth than the one others lived by. She was in the process of finding herself, Karin had thought, and listened indulgently and proudly to her explanations, believing it was how all young people should feel, as though the rules had been thrown overboard and it was up to them to make new ones. Now she realizes Helene must have had a broken heart at the time, and that she, her mother, didn't manage to see the difference. She looks across at Helene, who is smiling with a faraway look in her eyes while Ed whispers something in her ear. It's different to see it from the outside; it doesn't look like anything much, a hand on a thigh, the table behind bellowing 'You can't always get what you want' and thumping the beat with their fists. So dismal. Helene is like someone who's adrift, and all Karin wants is to save her.

'I thought you'd left,' Helene says when she sees her.

'I couldn't find a taxi.'

'I said she should come with us,' says Hailey, who has turned up behind her. 'You two left so fast.'

Ed has removed his hand.

'I thought you'd want to come back to the hotel now,' says Karin, looking at Helene.

'I'll stay a bit longer. But you can just go if you want to.'

Karin stands uncertainly in front of them. 'Can I have a word?'

Helene hesitates, but goes with Karin to the exit, folding her arms demonstratively. They stand right inside the door. Loose hairs swirl around Helene's face every time someone goes in or out. She has an obstinate look in her eyes.

'Has Endre called?' asks Karin.

Jack and Ant come in through the door with a cold waft of tobacco. 'Are you leaving?' says Jack.

'I'm not, but she is,' says Helene, pointing at Karin.

Karin gets two stiff hugs. They say that it's been nice meeting her and wish her a safe journey home, then go to the bar.

'I thought you of all people would understand,' says Helene. Her pupils are big and her jaw tense. 'It's so unfair.'

'What is?'

'I've never said a word about any of it.' Her bottom lip is quivering, but her eyes are dull and unfocused. It's as though her face is processing two different experiences at once. 'I know you were young, but I was just a little girl.'

'Oh.' Karin is silent for a few seconds. 'Is that what you're thinking about?' She doesn't know exactly what Helene is referring to, just that she has several accusations in mind. Actually, she's relieved. 'But you turned out fine, didn't you?' she says. 'Look at you.' Helene looks out towards the street, her jaw and throat forming a fine profile. You're beautiful, Karin thinks, and says it aloud, without thinking: 'You're beautiful.'

Helene's face contorts in distaste, as if she's been ordered to do something she doesn't want to. Something resembling contempt drifts over her like a shadow but then is eclipsed by a look of dejection. 'So what? Go back to the hotel and get some sleep. I'll see you in the morning.' She turns round and goes back to the table. Ed jumps up to let her past.

Then she's alone again. Something tightens round her throat like a dog collar, clouding her vision. She walks quickly, turns around a couple of times, but there's no one following her and there's nowhere she needs to be. It starts to drizzle. Restaurant and pub doors are sucked open from the inside; outside stand clusters of screeching people. Karin has to step down from the pavement into the road to avoid them, and each time she is filled with loathing. It's always like this, she thinks: the others stand their ground, hide in the crowd and expect her to be the one to move out of the way. She searches around for a taxi and sees a man jogging towards her with a tortured look on his face. He's wearing shorts and a vest, his thighs white and muscular, glistening with moisture. It's strange he's going for a run so late, is so exposed in a street full of party people, she thinks, but it's precisely this strangeness that makes her feel they are connected in a way, like lorry drivers who pass each other on a deserted stretch of road. She does her best to catch his eye, but he stares stiffly ahead, as if any contact with his surroundings would make him lose his composure.

She starts to look for a bar. Going to bed now, when all these people are awake, would be like letting them win. She hasn't done anything wrong. The place she finds in the end is big and run-down, with two floors joined by a wide staircase, and several snooker tables. It's not particularly nice. She asks for red wine, then changes her mind and orders a whisky soda. The bartender's arms are fat but strong and covered in colourful tattoos. She pays and finds a small table by the window. A snooker ball lands on the floor with a hard crack. 'You of all people.' That's what she'd said. 'I thought you of all people would understand.' But it's Helene who doesn't understand, Helene who categorizes Karin so she can sit at catered dinner parties with Endre's arm around her, saying: 'I grew up with a very distant mother.'

The summer holiday when Helene was four, Erik took her to his parents' place in the country, an architect-designed house by the sea, with relations staying in the surrounding cottages. They were going to be away for a week and Karin had asked not to go. While Erik packed, she had sat on the bed with Helene on her lap, hugging her little body and inhaling the smell of skin and children's shampoo. The next morning they got up early, as Erik wanted to avoid the worst of the traffic. Helene was grumpy and shoved Karin away when she tried to kiss her.

'She's just tired,' said Erik.

'I know,' said Karin.

At the time they were renting part of a large house, just outside the centre of Oslo. Most of the neighbours had gone on holiday, so she often had the garden to herself. After only a few days of being alone, she found herself forgetting her life usually contained other things. She quickly adopted new routines: toast and cut-up oranges for breakfast, evenings in front of the TV with rental videos, and a restless craving for fat and sugar which she practically never gave in to. She had planned to go jogging, to find new trails where she could run without thinking. Instead she slept, dozing off for anything between ten minutes and several hours, and woke up with sleep paralysis that she struggled out of by focusing on a toe or a finger.

Erik rang every day and they talked for a while before he passed the phone to Helene, who told her about crabs and soft ice and the big ticks they plucked with tweezers from the in-laws' two yellow Labradors. 'And then we exploded them,' she said, making the noise for Karin – which sounded wet, like an anticlimax.

Those first few times Helene suddenly hung up, Karin imagined Erik would call back to mark an official ending of the conversation. She waited, but he never rang.

The day before they were due to come home, she sat alone in a cafe in the city centre. She had a book in front of her and a half-eaten roll on a plate. The cafe was almost empty at midday. In one corner there was a couple; the man seemed to be in his twenties but the woman looked older. She showed off her strong legs in a short skirt, and picked prawns off the open sandwich the man was eating, dipping them in mayonnaise one by one. It made Karin think they didn't know each other particularly well, that the woman wanted to deny her sturdy body by eating very little.

After half an hour the woman got up, said something to the man and left. The man left soon after, without noticing Karin, but it turned out that he was going to buy cigarettes from the kiosk across the street. On the way back in he looked at her cheerfully, as though it was amusing she was sitting there. He ordered another coffee and smoked the whole time he drank it. Karin took her own packet of cigarettes out of her bag. Since Erik and Helene had left, she had smoked every day. Several times a day she would sit barefoot on the steps then go and throw the cigarette butts away in the dustbins behind the cast-iron gate. The soles of her feet were dirty and hard from walking across the gravel.

A loud, clattering noise made her turn towards the window. A postman was pulling a trolley behind him over the uneven tarmac. When she turned back, the man she had noticed was standing right in front of her. He was tall, with a coarsely chis-elled face: big nose, thick eyebrows, prominent chin. He wore a shapeless white T-shirt, baggy shorts and trainers. If it hadn't been for his shiny reddish lips, he wouldn't have had a single feminine feature. He pointed at her half-eaten roll. 'Don't you eat meat?' he said.

She glanced down at the slices of ham left on her plate. 'Yes,' she said. Karin wondered if he was waiting for her to eat the meat, put it into her mouth with her fingers and swallow it, but instead he asked if he could sit down. She didn't know why she said yes. He sat down opposite her and she pushed her plate towards him. 'Do you want it?' she said.

The man rolled up the ham and stuffed it into his mouth. He introduced himself as Finn, wiping his hand on his shorts before extending it across the table. His skin was cold and clammy. He asked if he could buy her another cup of coffee, and the way he said it made everything sound like a joke at her expense. She still said yes, though, one more time.

'But not here,' he said. 'Let's go somewhere else.'

She gathered her things together, put her book in her bag and followed him out. On the pavement outside he crouched down to tie his shoelace. She avoided looking at his fingers, as if they were doing something private.

He had done Film Studies, he said on the way. Now he worked nights at a psychiatric institution and lived in a flat-share in a part of town she rarely visited. He talked a lot and openly, telling her out of the blue that he had lost his father as a teenager. That made sense, Karin thought: he radiated so much serious masculinity it was almost childish, as though someone had told him at his most impressionable that he was the man of the house now. She said she was on holiday and was starting back at work the week after. 'Where do you work?' he asked.

'In a gallery,' she said.

He asked more questions: What kind of art did they sell? Did she like the pictures? What was the most expensive work she'd ever sold? What was the most difficult thing about the job? Had she ever lied to an artist or a customer?

'Here,' he said, stopping outside a pub.

He ordered a beer at the bar, and then it seemed silly to ask for coffee, so she did the same. He paid and carried both glasses to one of the tables out at the back surrounded by shrubs. He asked if she had been there before, which she hadn't, and he told her a moderately interesting story from his last visit. Their glasses came unstuck from the plastic tablecloth with wet sighs. After they had finished their drinks, he asked if she would like another beer. Karin hesitated but said yes, and he took back the empties. It made her feel safer, a sign he had good manners. While he was inside she went through everything she had said and done since they had left the cafe, and decided that the only thing she could be criticized for was her silence. The man sitting beside her was bolting down his food in front of a woman who insisted she wasn't hungry. 'I've already eaten,' the woman said, every time he offered her some.

Finn came back with two more glasses of beer. His fingers were long and slim with round joints, like a rope with knots. When the silence became too much, she did what she always did when she was nervous: described something in front of her as precisely as possible. She said aloud what she had thought about his hands, and that made him smile. He grasped her hand and studied it for a long time, pretending he could read palms. It was obvious he was using her stupid comment as an excuse to touch her. 'A long life,' he said, tracing one of the lines with his finger. 'Several love affairs.' He counted her fingertips. 'One, two, three, four, five kids. All of them boys.'

Karin had had her palm read once before, by a female teacher who spent social studies lessons talking about energies and showing them teaspoons she had bent with her mind. One double lesson she told the class that a male friend had once raped her on a camping trip. She described how she had left her body when it happened and watched the whole thing from above, how in the end her body gave up and stopped struggling. While the teacher spoke, it was as though she was hovering under the roof of the tent, and Karin pictured the whole class hovering up there with her, like ghosts on an excursion. Karin told the story to Finn, deliberately including all the details as if she was surprised she remembered them. He listened attentively, and Karin continued, describing how she later noticed that certain classmates got a glazed glimmer in their eyes when the teacher stood near them. She suspected they pictured themselves back there, hovering under the roof of the tent. 'It was an exciting place to be,' she said.

Finn's flat was big and chaotic. Lampshades hung right under the ceiling, shining an impersonal white light over the faces in there. There were several people seated round the sitting room table, and one of them was the woman from the cafe. She introduced herself as Dagny. It was the only name Karin registered, despite everyone shaking her hand when they introduced themselves, ever so politely. In the middle of the table there was a casserole dish and bowls with turmeric-yellow smears and lumps of rice. A couple of the boys' faces still glistened after the spicy meal. Karin smiled at all of them, and tried to quell a growing awkwardness by inhaling deeply.

Dagny had put on some make-up. Her broad cheekbones were matt with blusher, and around her eyes she had stuck small sparkly plastic crystals. 'Do you like my diamonds?' she said to Karin. 'I've got some for you too!'

She grabbed the tips of Karin's fingers and led her out of the sitting room and down a long hallway, with the same determination as when Helene wanted to show them something at nursery school. The room they came to was small, with red curtains that reached the floor. In one corner there was a mattress pushed up against the wall, with a duvet on top like a marzipan lid. On the left there was an open wardrobe with piles of clothes in metal baskets, and a full-length mirror leaning against the wall beside it. 'Is this your room?' asked Karin, and Dagny nodded as though it was obvious.

Plastic jewellery and pots of make-up lay scattered about. She told Karin to sit down in front of the mirror, and on the floor she found a hair clip and a clear plastic box with crystals stuck on a plastic sheet. Kneeling beside her, she gathered Karin's fringe in her hands and fastened it back with the clip. Her armpits smelled of sweet vinegar. 'You remind me of someone,' said Dagny. 'But I can't remember who. Have you always had a fringe?'

'Not always,' said Karin.

Dagny clicked open the plastic box with two fingers and studied the crystals. She chose a green one, struggling to get it onto her index finger so the sticky side was facing outwards. Then she leaned against Karin, pressed it hard against the outside of her eye, picked up a new one and continued the meticulous process. There was a copper bowl of incense next to the mirror; the sticks weren't lit but still gave off a faint, spicy scent, like in a church, enveloping Karin in something passive and pleasant. When Dagny had finished, she moved Karin's face firmly from side to side, finger and thumb over her chin. Then she took out her make-up bag again. The plastic tubes knocked against one another while she searched through them. 'Is this one okay?' she said, holding up a pink lipstick.

Karin nodded. Dagny leaned over again and rubbed the dry, waxy colour over her lips. Next, she moved to the side so Karin could see herself in the mirror. Her eyes were catlike, narrowed by the sparkling extensions. Her lips were big and pink.

The others had moved when they came back into the sitting room. Now they were sitting on two large sofas with a low table between them. A woven bamboo lampshade cast a patterned light on the walls; there were some wine bottles on the table and an LP sleeve covered in marijuana. Finn gestured to Karin to come and sit down beside him. He smiled at her but didn't comment on the make-up. She had already missed the moment in the cafe when the choice still lay ahead. Now the evening would follow a predictable pattern she couldn't escape from. Dagny sat down next to a thin guy with blonde curls who had two fingers missing on one hand. He said he had lost them as a child when he held his arm out of the car window and it slammed into a road sign. Karin wondered if that was true. She suspected the conversation had an underlying, reassuring layer she wasn't familiar with. Later on, Dagny took him into her room. Finn and Karin sat a bit longer, then they went into his room. The way he undressed was both confident and clumsy, as though he was alone in there.

The next day she woke up in her own bed. It was nearly twelve. Erik's bag lay beside Helene's little backpack in the kitchen, but she couldn't find them in any of the rooms. She made some coffee and took her cup with her into the bathroom. She was crouching down removing hair from the drain when she heard the front door open. Erik came in, shutting the door behind him. His hair was fairer from the sun.

'There you are,' she said.

He gave her a long kiss. She tucked in the corner of her towel where it was wrapped tight around her chest, to keep it in place. 'Had you been drinking?' he said.

She looked at him.

'Your clothes were in the hall,' he said. 'You'd just flung them there.'

'Where have you two been?'

'Just out to buy breakfast. I didn't want to wake you. Helene's been looking forward to seeing you.'

'Is she here?' said Karin. 'Helene?'

Karin leaves her scarf on the table and takes her handbag and the rest of her drink outside with her. Bar customers stand under the eaves with wet shoulders, smoking. She stands beside them, but not too close. Her lighter has stopped working; she shakes it a couple of times, holding her coat lapels together at the neck with her other hand. In the end she asks one of the men for a light. She listens half-heartedly to the conversation going on next to her, but doesn't understand what they're talking about. Something about a cat and a TV programme. They laugh loudly. She finishes her cigarette and then her drink in one swig, and takes the empty glass back inside. It's beginning to thin out, but there are still groups and couples sitting at some of the tables. No one looks up when she comes in. The bartender makes her another drink, warning her that it's her last. Karin smiles as steadily as she can, insisting that she isn't drunk. She gets a condescending look in return. 'No, no, honey,' the bartender says. 'We're closing soon.'

She continued seeing Finn the rest of that autumn. They usually met during the day or before his evening shifts began at the institution. She carefully analysed her own feelings but couldn't decide exactly what the attraction was. Perhaps it was as simple as him being different from Erik. The fact that he lay in the grass and didn't work out. He read Greek myths, talked about suicide as a 'philosophical dilemma' and preferred her to be passive when they slept together, which she liked. They kept a distance from each other that seemed tempting to reduce, without either of them actually trying. He came across as alternately wiser and much dimmer than her, and called her 'sexy brain', as if her brain was a thing he could see. They rarely made an effort to satisfy each other in ways that didn't give mutual pleasure simultaneously, and it occurred to her that neither of them was especially generous. And perhaps, she thought, that was what it was all about: being able to withhold something of yourself without consequences. It made her feel free.

She lost her job at the gallery, but soon afterwards was taken on in a small shop which sold conservative designer clothes. At night, if she woke up feeling agitated, she would ask Erik to lay his hand on her heart. He did so without a word, slipping his fingers under her top and holding his palm against her skin until the rhythm slowly but surely returned to normal. Every morning they had breakfast together. Erik was writing his thesis and spent a lot of time at the library. Karin said she wanted to start studying again. 'But then you need to apply,' said Erik. 'The academic year's started now.'

Twice she was called by other mothers saying that Helene was excluding children at nursery school, that she made rules for who could join in the games and who couldn't. She divided them into groups. When Karin asked what the rules involved, it was things like dark and fair hair, eye colour, nice and nasty. According to a book she had read, this was typical behaviour. The cognitive stage the children were at required that they made rules to cope with the abundance of information. It seemed hopeless to expect Helene to rise above this stage. She didn't say anything about this to the other mothers, just promised she would talk to Helene instead.

One day she came to pick her up at nursery school, the manager took her aside. She told her Helene had 'organized' a game involving kissing and showing the genitals, and that the children who didn't want to join in were excluded from the playhouse. Karin asked whether it was the excluding or the game that was the problem, and the manager replied that they would appreciate it if parents could talk to their children about 'which parts of the body are private'. If the nursery school hadn't been so conveniently close, Karin would have considered finding a new one. Still, with Helene sitting behind her on her bike, she pictured the dank darkness of the playhouse, the cylinder of dusty light from the only window and the circle of partially clothed children, with Helene standing in the middle like a deranged circus director. Erik laughed when she told him, but later he became very concerned.

'She's four years old,' said Karin. They were sitting at the kitchen table. There were dirty plates in the sink after Erik had made pasta. She had a knife in her hand and was slicing off flakes of Parmesan, which she ate straight from the blade. 'They made it sound like she'd been running a brothel in the centre of town.'

'I just don't see where she got it from,' said Erik.

'I guess they think young mothers are either religious or promiscuous and that both kinds produce sexually deviant children.'

Erik made a face. 'Don't say sexually. You said it yourself, she's four. It's not sexuality.'

'What is it then?'

'Just curiosity. Playing.' He picked a bit of cheese off the blade of the knife she held out to him and chewed it slowly. 'Once she wanted to sleep with Thumper between her legs. I said she couldn't, something about stuffed animals preferring to sleep with their head on the pillow, just like us. Maybe it's my fault.'

'Because you lied?'

'Because I planted the seed of shame in her. It can be the source of a lot of—'

'That sounds rather Freudian.'

'I just have this horrible feeling of having failed,' Erik said.

'Failed what?'

'I had the chance to break a pattern of behaviour, but I repeated it instead. It's how I was brought up, have I told you that? I got told off if they caught me rocking. I remember I told my mum I'd stopped because I wanted to make her happy, sort of take away the nasty stuff, and then she bought me an ice cream in the shop as a reward. Can you imagine?'

Karin had stopped eating and smiled. 'Rocking?'

'That's what they called it, and they said it wasn't good. But at least I was at proper school by then. Four is very early to start with that sort of thing, isn't it?'

Karin shrugged and suggested they could ask a paediatrician, but Erik said it certainly wasn't a medical problem. While he cleared away the rest of the meal, Karin washed up the saucepans and utensils that didn't go in the dishwasher. She was reminded of when, as a child, she had found her mother's only corset at the back of her drawer of rolled-up nylon stockings. She remembered how she had put it on while her mother was out, bending down and fastening the poppers between her legs. She viewed herself in the mirror for hours; she fetched raisins from the kitchen drawer and put them in her mouth one by one while she watched. The lace hung loosely over her flat chest. She had the vague feeling of intruding on something her mother had kept from her.

'You've never told me that,' she said. She dried her hands on the checked tea towel and hung it over the handle of the oven.

Erik turned towards her. He was crouched down in front of the low fridge, making room for the Tupperware container of leftovers. 'Hmm?'

'How you were brought up. You've never told me.'

'No. Nor have you,' said Erik. 'No one wants it to be used against them, I suppose.'

Before they went to bed, they watched a film on the sofa. They started to have sex, but stopped after a few minutes. It suddenly seemed repulsive to express their desires.

It has stopped raining, but it's still dripping from the rooftops. She notices she's unsteady as she walks, and has problems imagining the external gaze on herself, which she normally uses to fine-tune her behaviour. She stops outside a closed restaurant to check her phone and sees the battery is flat. Out of the corner of her eye, she notices some boys on the other side of the street and recognizes the shiny bomber jackets. It's the gang who bummed cigarettes and started the row with Jack. One of them shouts something at her, but she shakes her head, smiles and carries on walking. He crosses the road and she hears his steps behind her. He wants to know where she's going, if she has more cigarettes to give away. Without stopping she holds out the packet behind her, saying he can take as many as he wants, that she's on her way home. He takes one, walking faster so he's soon beside her, and asks for a light. The glare from the street lights sways in front of her, and the sound of her shoes on the pavement is strangely loud and irregular. He looks like he's in his early twenties, maybe younger. He has a greasy fringe and a patch of hard spots along his jaw. 'Give it to me,' he says.

She gives him the lighter and he shakes it a few times, as if there's a knack to it. They have both stopped walking, apparently waiting for the other to do something. She notices he's studying her eyes and tries her best to focus. He sniffs, wiping his nose on the back of his hand. Then he tells her to wait; he's going to get a light from his mate, he says. She shakes her head again, says it's fine, that she's on her way home. 'Take the packet,' she says, but he just repeats that she must wait.

'Why don't you want to talk to a stranger?' he says. 'Scared something will happen?'

He comes back with a lit cigarette between his lips. He uses it to light another, which he gives to her. She takes it and thanks him, although technically it's hers. It's as though the situation has absorbed some of her intoxication; it seems unsteady and absurd, while she herself feels clear-headed. It's difficult to know what the boy wants, but it occurs to her that she might have landed in a dangerous predicament. She remembers how he leaned towards her outside the corner shop, his mocking, burning eyes. At the same time she feels something else, a kind of relief, perhaps. She starts to walk, but slows down not to appear rude. He follows her.

One Saturday she was with Finn at a pub. It was winter, and Erik had taken Helene to the mountains to teach her downhill skiing with a friend and his two children. A group of older men were holding a wake further inside. Finn had some pills, which they took before their second drink. When the drugs started to kick in, she examined herself in the cracked mirror behind the bar. The look in her eyes was unfamiliar and captivating, and waves of warmth crashed through her. There were orders of service from the funeral with a picture of the deceased scattered around, and two aluminium trays of finger food on one of the tables. Karin and Finn had small, shiny sausages on napkins in front of them, gifts from the mourners. She stroked his thigh. He wrinkled his nose, saying she shouldn't use perfume, and in the toilet she rubbed it off her neck with wet paper towels. His cool tongue twisted in her mouth, chilled by his cold drink. Their cigarettes burned down to the filters without them taking a single drag. She burned a hole in her skirt, stuck her finger through it and made it bigger, exposing a circle of goose-pimpled flesh. They got more drinks. A drunk man in a suit put his arm around them and asked Finn what he was waiting for; life was short, he said, and 'children are a blessing!'

'I don't think I'm the type,' said Karin, and none of them protested.

The next morning she stood in the bathroom at Finn's wearing one of his T-shirts. The basin was clogged up with bits of soap and there were cotton buds with yellow tips on the floor beside the bin. She could hear him moving around in his room next door. She lifted the T-shirt with one hand and sat down on the toilet, reaching across to turn on the tap.

'There are two kinds of people,' he said when she came back in, shutting the door behind her. 'The ones who piss with the tap on and the ones who piss with the door open.'

He was lying in bed. His chest looked concave between his broad shoulders, and she went over and laid her face against it. It was obvious he thought the latter were best, or at least more liberated, and therefore something to strive for. That provoked her.

Later on they watched a film about a woman on the run called Wanda. In an early scene Wanda stands before a judge in a small courtroom with her husband, a miner, who has asked for a divorce. Her blonde hair is done up in rollers under a white scarf. The husband has stated his complaints to the court: he must make his own breakfast, she doesn't take care of the housework or the children, doesn't bother to do anything, just lies on the sofa all day. Wanda doesn't protest. On a bench in the background, you can see the two little children sitting on the lap of another woman who is looking after them, the husband's new girlfriend. Wanda doesn't so much as glance at them. Finn thought it was a fantastic scene. He crouched down to rewind the video, pointing out how the director, a woman, let the camera dwell on Wanda's passive face. A more sentimental film-maker would have kept the children in shot, he said. He poured them some more wine. So many feminists were wrong about this film, he said; Wanda's passivity wasn't a sign of weakness but of integrity. She could accept society as it was, but only if she stood on the outside. 'Do you get it?' he said, and went back to the video player to rewind the film again.

The air got warmer. It smelled of mown grass and hot tarmac. Boats were put back on the water, then lilies of the valley appeared. Life trundled on with its small, everyday transformations and with Helene at the centre. The garden furniture they shared with the neighbours was carried out onto the lawn in front of the house. On the way home from nursery school Karin and Helene would pick bunches of small blue and white woodland flowers, and fill the sitting room and bedrooms with them in glasses of water. Erik sat in the library all day writing his thesis. He would come home red-eyed and was moved by the slightest thing: by hearing Helene list all the names of flowers she had learned by heart, or being told he liked butter when she held a buttercup under his chin and saw its yellow reflection in his unfamiliar stubble. For her birthday Helene was given a book about flowers by Karin's mother, who thought Helene had got her interest in flora from herself. 'She's five,' said Karin. 'She's interested in everything.'

Helene still struggled socially at nursery school; she was either the boss or everyone's enemy. On the days Karin didn't work she fetched Helene early and took her to a cafe, where they had cinnamon buns and chocolate-coated almond slices. One day they went to the science and technology museum and, as they walked home, they chatted about what they had seen. It had been raining and Helene dragged a pink umbrella behind her on the tarmac. Karin couldn't be bothered to ask her to stop, and it got ruined. They passed a playground that was closed; they just had to open the gate to go in. The slide was too wet, but Karin used the sleeve of her sweater to dry the swings, two decrepit car tyres with a kind of nappy for the smallest children to put their legs through. When it was Helene's turn to push, Karin held the chains and lay back her head, so her hair tickled Helene's face and made her laugh. 'You're gorgeous,' said Helene, with her hands entangled in Karin's hair.

'Gorgeous?' Karin smiled. Clouds floated past in the sky, slipping away from each other like emerging continents. 'Where have you learned that?' She lifted Helene onto her lap, pushed off in the wet sand and stretched out her legs in a straight line. They rocked slowly back and forth.

When they came home, they made tomato soup with macaroni, kicked off their slippers and sat on top of the kitchen table singing to the cress on the windowsill to make it grow faster. In the morning Helene screamed that she wanted to brush her hair herself, and Karin let her. It was like that the whole time: she wanted to do it herself. Choose what to wear, open the bottle of fluoride, use the blender, carry her backpack. Karin remembered what the midwife had said when Helene was born: 'She'll grow more like you,' she'd said. 'Just wait and see.'

The street lights gradually disappear. The boy asks where she's from. She answers that she's from Norway, and he wants to know if it's true that a beer costs ten pounds there. 'More or less,' she says.

The road they're walking down has ended in a residential area. The corner shops and pubs have gone, and on both sides of the street restored Victorian houses loom above them, shrouded in darkness like a gothic tableau. Cars are parked with two wheels on the pavement and several times she has to squeeze against the brick wall to get past. She says to the boy that she must turn back, that she needs a taxi. He asks again where she's going. She says she's going back to the hotel and he asks where it is, saying he has a mate who can give her a lift.

'It's fine,' says Karin.

'Relax,' he says, holding out his palms. 'It's not a van we're talking about. He drives an Uber.'

Karin repeats that it's fine and says she's going to meet her daughter. They've agreed to go back together, she says, with as much conviction as she can muster. He looks her up and down, then shrugs.

'It was just an offer,' he says. 'Only trying to be polite.'

His bomber jacket is a little too short; she can see the white belt holding up his jeans and his boxer shorts bulging out. He asks if she's married. Karin says yes. She sees the lights of the first corner shop a bit further on, and cars turning at a crossroads. She feels a tug at her coat; he holds her by the elbow and asks why she's walking so fast.

'You think I'm going to hurt you?' he says. 'Is that what you think?'

It was nearly summer. They bought trainers with Velcro for Helene, who refused to take them off, even inside. After she had fallen asleep, they had to wiggle them off her little feet, which kept retreating under the duvet like the heads of frightened tortoises. At weekends they went for walks in the forest; they would take the metro and walk up to the top of Vettakollen, nodding silently at other families who passed by. Helene struggled to climb over the big stones, but she was keen. Erik called her a mountain goat, and timed her with the hands on his watch. One time Karin walked behind them for a while, but then she was overcome with a burning desire to wear herself out. She jogged past them, ignoring Helene's cries that she wanted to go first. Dripping with sweat at the top, she cooled her face with water from the marsh. When Helene and Erik arrived, she apologized. They sat down on a large rock with a view of the whole of Oslo, and had chocolate and nectarines and strawberry squash. They tried to find their house, the nursery school and the town hall.

Soon after Midsummer's Eve, Erik went to his parents' place in the country with Helene. Karin was going to come down by bus after work a couple of days later.

She lay in the park with Finn's head on her lap, thighs sticky where they met under his thick hair. He went on about books and articles he had read, about friends of friends who did things he respected, about ideas he had for films and new companies. He spoke about his father, about leukaemia being hereditary, and said he sweated a lot at night. Karin pulled up handfuls of grass by the roots and let them fall back down in the same place, so they lay on the ground like a toupee.

Seized with sentimentality and something else, maybe haste, she took him to a small lake where she had spent countless summer days as a child, where there were dead bodies dumped on the bottom that swam up and grabbed you by the ankles if you were in the water too long. Finn threw himself into the lake naked, and afterwards they drank beer and fondled each other under the towel. She picked and named all the flowers she recognized from Helene's book. Later on they went back to Finn's place, and sat in the sitting room with Dagny and some other people. Karin said very little, as usual, and was longer in the kitchen than necessary when she went to make some tea.

'It's weird you've got a kid,' said Finn.

They lay dozing and contented on his bed. He stroked her stomach, tracing circles with his finger round her navel. She smiled, following his movements with her eyes. 'Why?' she said.

'Because you're the type who makes tea without asking if anyone else wants some.'

She sat up.

'Don't be cross,' he said. 'I didn't mean it like that. It's good you don't go round taking care of everyone. It's just something that occurred to me.'

She found her elastic band in the folds of the duvet and gathered her hair into a ponytail. He tried to pull her back down onto the bed, but she wouldn't move. She didn't know why she was reacting as strongly as she was. It was as though what she had thought was a mirror had actually been a window, that a part of him had sat observing her and come to conclusions she didn't know anything about. It was unbearable.

'Why are you angry?' he said. 'It's a good thing.'

'I'm not angry,' she said. 'It's humiliating.'

Then he smiled, looking relieved, and stroked her cheek with his finger. 'Forget it,' he said. 'It doesn't matter. Don't be embarrassed.'

'That's not what I mean,' she said. She put on her T-shirt. 'I mean that you point it out, that you go round thinking about what I'm like.'

Now he sat up too. He looked at her. 'But don't you think about what I'm like?'

'I'm too busy examining my own faults.'

. . .

They have stopped walking and are standing close together on the narrow pavement. They're alone, and the windows in the nearest house are dark. Karin says once again that she must go home, that her husband is lying awake in the hotel room. She tries to ease her elbow out of his grasp, but carefully, so as not to provoke him and make the situation more threatening than it needs to be. Then he comes even closer. He's surprisingly strong. His face is almost touching hers, and his breath feels warm against her cheek. His mouth smells of beer, but also something sweet and sour, like lime. She prepares herself, noticing how her tense her body is.

'Got any money?'

Something serious has come over him now, and that makes her feel safer. It suddenly seems like he wants this to be over as much as she does. She opens her wallet and sees that she has just over a hundred pounds in notes, what's left of the amount she took out at the airport. She hands him the biggest one, a fifty-pound note. He takes it and asks if she's got any more. Further up the road, two people go into the corner shop. Karin shakes her head, saying it's all she's got. He looks at her, coming even closer. Maybe her voice would carry far enough. He reaches towards her face as if he's going to grab it. Then he closes his fingers around the dangling earrings she has put on to look smart, and pulls them out of the holes with one swift tug.

Several weeks went by without her seeing Finn. A month, then two. Several times Erik answered the phone and said hello into the receiver – 'Hello? Hello?' – before hanging up with a shrug. 'Probably one of the neighbours' kids,' he said. 'Or a nutter. Next time you should answer and we'll see if he does some heavy breathing.'

Nursery school started again and Helene brought friends home. While they played, Helene kept turning towards her mother as if to check she was paying attention, and was excessively sweet until she had suddenly had enough and wanted her friends to go home. When one of them was picked up, the mother turned out to be a woman Karin knew from the short time she spent in a postnatal group. Karin invited her in for coffee and they agreed to do it again.

At weekends she made sandwiches and filled bottles with squash, watched Erik play doubles tournaments or walked to tourist cabins in the forest, with a change of clothes in her backpack so Helene wouldn't get cold on the way back. She started to feel like a normal person again, with a life that required difficult but normal decisions for it to work. One rainy Sunday Erik's tournament was moved inside a hall. Karin couldn't bear the sweaty atmosphere, the sound of balls whacking against the walls, so she took Helene to a cafe instead. 'We'll come back for the prize-giving,' she said, but Erik said they didn't need to.

She didn't see Finn until after they had sat down. She was busy keeping Helene quiet beside her, making sure she didn't knock over her apple juice when she reached for the crayons. Finn was with Dagny, who was already on her way over to them. He came after her hesitantly, his arms hanging loosely by his side.

'Karin!' Dagny bent down and hugged her. She was wearing a tiny pair of shorts with frayed edges that danced around the top of her legs.

Helene looked up uncertainly at the unfamiliar faces and lay her elbows protectively over her drawing.

Dagny went round to Helene's side of the table, knelt and asked if she could see the picture: 'Please.'

Helene looked at Karin, who tried to smile even though her body was boiling over. So many of her feelings appeared initially as temperature changes.

'It's Bastian,' said Helene.

'The police chief?' said Dagny. 'I saw that straight away.'

Finn said nothing. He stared at Karin, then at Helene. He went to buy some coffee.

'We'll join you,' said Dagny. She asked if she could have some paper too. Helene gazed at Dagny as she helped herself to crayons and at the lifelike shapes she created on the white sheet. When Dagny requested help, Helene pushed her own drawing towards Karin, leaned over the paper with Dagny and nodded when she was asked if the princess should have a crown. Dagny was brown from the sun, and their bare arms lying next to each other were like stripes in a box of Neapolitan ice cream.

When Karin tried to wipe some egg custard off Helene's cheek with a napkin, she yelled furiously and hit Karin's outstretched arm with her own. Finn turned round in the queue and his eyes met Karin's. He wanted to talk to her back at his place, he said, but Karin said she couldn't leave Helene. Dagny said she could look after her. She said she had colouring things and dressing-up clothes in her room, that children always loved her, and that she had a niece Helene's age. When Karin hesitated, Dagny rolled her eyes, crouched down in front of Helene and asked if she liked drawing with glitter gel pens. Helene didn't answer. 'Karin, don't be silly,' Dagny said and took Karin's arm, scraping her bare skin with her nails. 'I'll look after her.'

When they got to the flat, Karin explained to Helene that she would just be gone for a little while, less than an episode of her favourite children's TV programme, that she was going to talk to her friend. 'I'll be back in a minute,' she said.

Helene nodded and took Dagny's hand. As they disappeared down the hallway, Karin could hear Helene telling Dagny about a game she had at home. It felt like a stab in her heart knowing Helene could so quickly get attached to Dagny as soon as she herself was out of sight.

There were three boys sitting at the kitchen table drinking. Instinctively she looked towards the door, but Finn whispered that she should relax. He said hi to the boys and led Karin through the sitting room. She could already look back at everything to do with this flat as being in the past. When they reached his room, he closed the door behind him. As soon as he started talking, she knew there wasn't any more to say, and she was tired of his voice. She still let him kiss her. It seemed appealing to surrender all power just before she made a final decision.

Afterwards, she didn't know how much time had passed. She quickly got dressed and pinned back her hair in front of the mirror. Finn put his arms round her from behind, with his threadbare boxer shorts sagging on his hips, but she wriggled out of his grasp. The decision she had made only an hour or so earlier to go back to Finn's and let Dagny look after Helene seemed completely foreign to her. All she wanted was to go home with Helene, but Dagny's bedroom was empty. The door stood open and on the floor there was toilet paper decorated with black squiggles. It smelled sickly sweet, like rotten fruit. On the bed lay a crocheted silver dress with the price tag still on it. The bedside table overflowed with bottles and glasses, and by the mirror there was an overturned ashtray shaped like an exotic shell. 'They're probably in the kitchen,' said Finn behind her.

They weren't in the kitchen. The three boys who had been sitting there earlier had gone too. Karin asked Finn if he knew who was home, who was in the flat, but he didn't. She went from room to room opening doors, but apart from a guy in a vest and basketball shorts engrossed in a nature programme without sound, the flat was empty. Karin went back to Dagny's room and idiotically checked behind the door and under the duvet. 'Where is she?'

'How should I know?' said Finn. 'Maybe they've gone out.'

'Why would Dagny take Helene out?' she said.

He didn't answer. She realized that all the experiences they'd had together were entirely worthless. Possible scenarios filled her head. Panic made time go slower. Helene's white Velcro trainers were still by the front door. She picked them up and stood holding them in her hands like two defibrillator paddles. Then she heard noises from the bathroom at the end of the hall. The door was shut but opened when Karin touched the handle. The basin was full of make-up and things that had fallen out of the open medicine chest. There was a broken glass on the tiled floor. Helene sat alone and fully dressed in the corner of the shower grasping a bottle of shampoo. The shower curtain was partly pulled across. She looked up at Karin. She was wearing Dagny's pink lipstick. Karin took four quick steps towards her, pulled her up by the arm and started rubbing the colour off her lips with so much force that her finger scraped Helene's milk teeth. The colour was smudged from the corners of her mouth across her cheeks.

'What on earth are you doing?' said Finn from the doorway.

Helene said nothing, just kept staring at Karin with wide-open eyes.

Karin is woken by the sound of someone talking to her. It's a man. The words coming out of his mouth make no sense. She asks him to speak more slowly. 'What have I done?' she says. 'I haven't done anything.'

In the end she realizes he's speaking English. 'Miss,' he says. 'Please.' She's in London. She's sitting in a taxi and has fallen asleep on the way. The driver looks at her patiently. He has a dyed red beard and a small, white hat. His clothes are white too. 'This is where you wanted to go,' he says, pointing down a street towards the hotel. 'I can't get any closer.'

When Karin and Helene came home, the little silver trophy was standing on the chest of drawers in the hall. The flat smelled fresh and Erik was sitting barefoot on the sofa, straight from the shower. On the way home Karin had wondered if Helene would remember the experience, if as an adult she would recall the time she was left alone with strangers. It had gone fine, everything pointed to that, but Karin's actions had had nothing to do with the outcome. It was a disturbing but liberating thought. It was Erik who put Helene to bed that night, and afterwards they sat at the kitchen table as usual. She told him about Finn, the most important details. As soon as Karin had said what she had to say, it was as though her brain stopped working. Even Erik's reaction was delayed. When it came, she observed him as if in a dream, with everything out of proportion. His body collapsed dramatically, then regained a dignified calm. He called her a bitch, a word she had never heard him use before, and it sounded fake and theatrical in his mouth. 'I want you to leave,' he said finally, but she had already got up.

It was windy out, and her hair was tossed against her eyes and cheekbones. The trees along the street were swaying calmly. She wasn't wearing much and her feet were only in sandals. The leather soles slapped against the pavement as she walked. She turned round, but the road was empty behind her. She kept switching between slow and fast steps, unable to decide the pace; she wanted to be overpowered by the drama of the

124

moment, by rupture and movement. She considered crying, but as soon as the thought occurred to her she admitted to herself that it would have to be an active decision on her part and that tears would make her feel self-conscious. Despite everything, she was in surprisingly good spirits. For the first time in her life she saw everything clearly. It was as if she had found her way out of a maze, stepped out of the shade into sun against her skin and endless countryside. She could lie down, and no one would tell her to get up.

She locked eyes with a white-haired woman who was changing a candle in her window. Karin could make out a TV on behind her in an over-furnished sitting room. While she looked out, the woman held the candle firmly so it would stand in the wax from the old one. From where she stood, it must have looked like Karin was on her way somewhere.

Karin is floating, like a soul waiting to enter a body. It's a moment she likes, the daily fraction of a second before she comes round and slips out of that room of endless possibilities.

In the bathroom she fills glass after glass with water from the tap. In the mirror, lines from the pillow crisscross her wrinkles in a sloppy network. A small window above the toilet lets in the sound of cars and distant activity. She leaves the tap to run and splashes cold water on her face. A pain is spreading between her eyes. She finds her handbag on the floor next to the bed and looks for painkillers. There are two loose paracetamol tablets in the little pocket with lip balms and hair elastics, and she picks off bits of fluff before she swallows both of them with what's left of the water she bought at Heathrow. PURE LIFE BEGINS NOW, it says in blue letters on the plastic bottle.

The room smells of sleep and exhaled alcohol. She goes over to the window and pulls back the curtains. It's cloudy. A woman in white trousers is struggling to get a boy into the back seat of a low car without touching his muddy wellies. Karin calls reception and asks for some coffee, but they don't offer room service. She finds her phone under her pillow and plugs it into the charger. She's got two messages from Endre. *Hi Karin*, the first one says. *Is Helene with you?* It was sent at half past three in the morning. The next one, sent at nine, says: *Forget it, I got through to her*, and a yellow smug-looking smiley. Torstein has rung seven times altogether and sent two messages just saying: *Answer*. She deletes the missed calls and messages and in the end also his number. The thought that she called him, in that forced upbeat voice, makes her physically ill. She pulls off her underwear and gets in the shower.

Afterwards she sits on the bed, cracking her toes against the carpet. She doesn't feel well. She cries as much as she can, until there are no more tears, then she loosens the towel she has wrapped round her hair and presses it against her eyes. She picks up her phone again and sends a message to Helene. *Good morning*, she writes. She wants to write *Where are you?* but is afraid of insinuating something that would make Helene cross. She pictures her naked, sitting on the edge of a bed with her hair tangled at the back of her neck, listening to Ed clattering around in the kitchen – suddenly a complete stranger. And who is Karin then? She's a stranger too.

It's ten already, and the lecture begins in an hour. She leans back, feeling a stiffness in her thighs.

There's a knock at the door. Helene is fully dressed, standing there with two coffees in her hands. Her eyes are bright and clear, even if her skin lacks its usual glow. She looks great. She hands one of the cups to Karin and walks past her into the room. 'It's actually a bit bigger than mine,' she says, looking around. 'I'm not kidding.'

She tries to drag the massive chair from under the desk with one hand, gives up, puts down her coffee and uses both hands. Karin stands there, wondering if she should get dressed, but she doesn't want to in front of Helene; she can't change in the bathroom either, as it would be odd to shut the door behind her, like a bashful teenager. She sits down on the bed, holding her coffee tightly on her lap. It leaves a scalding ring on her thigh.

'I left soon after you,' says Helene.

'Oh,' says Karin. She sips her coffee.

'So maybe it was stupid not to share a taxi.'

'I'm sure it was nice for you to be alone with your friends, without me.'

Helene nods. They can hear someone walking above them, a vacuum cleaner being turned on. 'Nothing happened,' says Helene after a while. 'Between Ed and me, even if it maybe looked that way. We used to go out together, you probably realized that, but nothing happened, yesterday, I mean.'

'I didn't think—'

'Yes you did, I could see you did.'

'He seems like a nice man, Ed.'

'Does he?' says Helene.

'Did you manage to talk to Endre?'

Helene looks right at her. 'Why are you so bothered about me talking to Endre? Why can't you just be on my side?'

Karin presses her thighs together self-consciously. 'I didn't know there were sides,' she says. 'But of course I'm on yours.'

'No you're not. You're always playing everyone off against everyone else.'

'What's that supposed to mean?'

Helene lifts her cup towards her mouth. The plastic lid isn't on properly and coffee splashes down the white shirt she's wearing. She jumps up, still holding the cup. She makes a strange, half-strangled gurgling noise. Tears roll from her tightly closed eyes. 'Fuck, fuck, fuck,' she says. 'Why can't anyone do their job properly and take just a tiny bit of pride in their work? What's wrong with people?' She holds her shirt away from her front and blows down it.

Karin hurries into the bathroom, dampens a towel in cold water and runs back, but then stands there helplessly with the wet end a few centimetres from Helene's chest. Something stops her.

Helene takes the towel from her and presses it firmly against the damp patch. The shirt material darkens and the lace underneath becomes visible. 'This is no good,' she says, after some seconds of silence. She dries her eyes with the back of her hand, wipes under her eyelashes with her finger and sits down despondently with the towel on her lap. 'I think I've burned myself,' she says. She unbuttons her shirt and takes it off. The skin above her left breast is red. Her bra is see-through and her breasts hang heavily over the wires. She strokes the red mark with her finger.

'Do you want to borrow something of mine?' says Karin cautiously.

'No, it's okay. I've got clothes in my room. I'll go and change. We must leave soon if we're going to make the lecture.'

'You still want to go?' says Karin.

'Yeah,' says Helene. She starts to get up.

'It's not so easy,' says Karin. 'You seem so confident about everything you do.'

Having bent down to get her shirt, Helene now stops and sits up again in disbelief, as though she's been insulted. 'Me?' she says. 'If there's anyone here who thinks they've got all the answers, it's you. You're the one who refuses to fit in, acting like you're above everything and everyone the whole time.'

It's as though the words have been lying ready inside her. It's similar to how she started talking as a child. 'You're very angry,' says Karin.

Helene picks up her shirt from the floor and starts to put it on. She says nothing. Karin strokes the duvet beside her. 'I never demand anything,' she says.

'And you think that's generous? It's nothing. Nada.' Helene looks down at herself. She seems to finally give up the idea of a clean white shirt. She lifts her coat from the back of the chair and lays it over her arm. 'Are you coming?'

Karin nods. They arrange to meet at reception in quarter of an hour.

Helene walks towards the door, then turns round as if there's something she's forgotten. 'I've been so worried that I'm just like you,' she says.

Erik forgave her. When she came home the next morning, he was still sitting in the kitchen. He was angry, extremely hurt, but he thought they could get through it. It would involve a lot of work, he said, but he was willing to try. What else could they do? Karin moved out the week after, first to her mother's, where he turned up and punched a hole through a plaster wall in the hall. In the end he calmed down, drifting into a mild, bewildered apathy. He said that the most important thing now was to think about Helene.

'I know,' said Karin.

'Do you?' he said. 'Or are you just saying that?'

She found a small flat in central Oslo, but Erik said that if she lived there Helene couldn't stay the night. She moved again, and went out by herself in the evenings. For a while the plan was to share custody of Helene equally. They stuck to this arrangement for a year and a half, handing her over each

Sunday, calling and complaining when the other one was late. But as time passed, it seemed simpler for Karin to bring Helene back a few days early, to return to the life she lived when she was alone.

Just before she turned thirty, she felt a nostalgic urge to categorize everything and everyone that had affected her existence. She wrote lists and slept with men she had slept with earlier, in the hope of being preserved and regenerated through their gaze. When she rang Finn, he told her that he was married and working as a teacher at the film school but would like to have a beer. They slept together at her place. He said Dagny lived in Tromsø, that she had children with an older dramatist and was a make-up artist at a local theatre. They saw each other several times after that. Before it ended for the second time, he dipped two fingers in cocaine and stuck them inside her, holding them there while he revealed what he had done, how quickly the drug entered the bloodstream from the vagina.

When Helene was twelve, she said she wanted to stop living with Karin during the week, that it was tiring to pack. She was supposed to come every other weekend, but the visits became more and more sporadic. At the age of thirty-three Karin had her first abortion; she had her second when she was thirty-nine. She moved in with various men, but it never lasted long: five years with an unassuming social worker was the longest. Once in a while she would introduce someone to Helene, but she usually came alone to birthday parties and celebrations at the home of Erik and Imke, the German anaesthetist he married. For two years she was with a man who owned a catering company, a man who sat drinking after work and then with a cold stare insisted that she must have been abused as a child, even though she repeated ad nauseam that she hadn't. 'I can see it in your eyes,' he said. 'Who was it?

Your father? An uncle? A neighbour? You can tell me. Just say it. Why won't you tell me?'

When she asked him why he couldn't believe her, he started to cry.

It's drizzling again. Karin and Helene walk along the streets in silence. Now and then Helene takes her phone out of her pocket to check they're going the right way. They're running late, but still stop off at a cafe so Helene can buy another coffee. She seems nervous. Karin says they probably have coffee at the festival, but then Helene looks at her stupidly, saying 'people like that' don't touch caffeine. Karin waits under the green awning. Through the window she can see Helene talking to someone in the queue, a woman.

She thinks about the boy from last night with a gnawing feeling in her stomach. She pictures her earrings on the fleshy earlobes of an over-made-up girlfriend. She thinks about one of her father's stories that he loved to tell, about when at the age of nine she dropped his wallet in the sea. It was in the summer; he was going to take her out in the sailing boat, and he gave her his wallet so it wouldn't fall out of his back pocket when he undid the mooring line. Then he told her to take the rope, presumably with her free hand, but in a moment of confusion she dropped the wallet when she reached for the rope, and saw it sink slowly to the bottom of the sea. Her father loved to tell this story; he thought it said something about who she was. What she actually remembered best was when they finally came out onto the open sea. The wind had subsided and they had to use the engine instead, a sweet, humming sound mixed with seagull cries. She told him stories about marine animals and mermaids, and when the engine packed up and he lost his temper, she stared silently and respectfully towards the horizon. She remembered it as a lovely day. And still, when he was going to tell a story about who she was, this was what he remembered: that she dropped what she was supposed to hold.

Helene comes out of the cafe with the woman Karin saw her talking to in the queue. They wish each other a nice day and walk off in opposite directions, but when the woman has gone a few metres she spins round enthusiastically.

'Now I remember!' she calls out. 'It's one of the mothers at my son's nursery school. Textile artist, Irish. Really nice.' She looks relieved, waves before she turns round again, and walks on.

'It happens all the time,' says Helene to Karin. 'People tell me I look like someone they know, an old girlfriend or the hairdresser they went to before they moved from their home town. As if it's a compliment.'

'I hear that too,' says Karin. 'That I look like people. Maybe it means you look like me?'

As soon as she has said it, she remembers Helene's comment a bit earlier. It's not meant as a response, but she realizes it might seem like it is. She opens her mouth to say something else, then closes it. Helene looks at Karin as if she's a screen showing an incomprehensible email, then hands her a paper bag. Inside there's a croissant. Helene takes her own one out with a white napkin and drops the bag in a bin.

The yoga festival is in a concrete and glass building, on an asphalted square with several similar buildings. They arrive half an hour after the lecture was supposed to begin. It turned out that the entrance was in a different street from the one marked on the map. At one point Helene had stopped, crouched down and given up, so Karin had to take over the phone. Outside there are flags and posters confirming they have come to the right place. It seems to be a relatively small event, and there's no sign of anyone either inside or out. 'Shall we go in?' says Karin.

The lobby is large and the ceiling high. A grey carpet has been rolled out and at the end of it there's a young girl sitting behind a makeshift reception, two desks shoved together, with piles of paper and brochures in front of her. She's eating cut-up fruit from a plastic container, but puts it to one side when she sees them coming over. Helene takes out her phone and searches for the tickets in her inbox, while the girl smiles at Karin. She has light brown hair in a thick plait and is wearing sports gear.

'Has the lecture started?' asks Karin.

The girl looks down at the sheet of paper where the programme is printed. She asks which lecture they want to go to, and when Karin says the name of it she nods, saying that it's been going on for a while but that they can just go in. 'Third door on the left,' she says. 'There's a sign.'

They each get a sticker and are asked to put it on their chests so it's visible.

'Enjoy the festival!' the girl calls after them, and it sounds hollow in the big empty room.

'Maybe this was a bad idea,' says Helene as they walk across the carpet in the hall. They can hear the faint sound of a woman's voice in a microphone.

'We'll just go and see,' says Karin.

The door is shut, but Charlotte's name and the title of the lecture are written in capital letters on a laminated sign. Karin opens the door carefully and creeps inside, with Helene behind her. The room is surprisingly big, like an auditorium in a cinema, with the stage on ground level and rows of chairs slanting upwards. The entrance is partly hidden behind the stairs, so they can only see Charlotte and the first rows of the audience. She's standing in the middle of the stage talking enthusiastically into a microphone. She's wearing white trousers, a white woollen sweater and beige ankle boots. Her blonde hair is tied back and she has a yellow, metallic scarf round her neck. 'It's a very Western idea,' she says, 'that you should be free to give and receive love without making a commitment. Very individualistic. In the East they have a completely different view.'

She drinks from a glass of water on a high folding table. It seems like the lecture is over; the screen behind her shows a photo of a fence with an open gate and fields behind it, and at the top it says THANK YOU SO MUCH in black writing, and then a smiley.

'Any more questions?' she says. 'Yes, you in the turquoise. Can someone please pass her the microphone?'

There's a sound of people moving, mumbling and low chatter, then it's quiet.

'I've suffered some big losses recently,' says a mild female voice. 'But I've worked a lot with myself and meditation has helped me a great deal, I think. But lately I've been wondering…' There's a pause. 'How can you tell the difference between peace of mind and numbness?'

Charlotte lays her hand on her heart. 'First of all, I'm sorry for all you've been through,' she says. 'We all are, aren't we? And we love you, that's the most important thing.' She looks round the room, nodding. 'So to your question.'

Helene has been holding the door ajar, but now it slams shut. Charlotte turns in their direction. 'Those of you standing in the doorway, just come in and sit down,' she says. She shields her eyes with one hand not to be dazzled by the stage lights. 'There's a few empty seats by the aisle here. Please come in.'

Several faces in the front rows turn round.

Helene grabs hold of Karin. 'Forget it, let's go.'

'Are you sure?' asks Karin, but Helene's already on her way out.

Karin hurries after her down the hall. The girl who welcomed them a few minutes ago looks surprised and asks if everything's all right, but Helene continues out of the door and doesn't slow down until they're standing on the pavement. 'I just remembered I need to get my dress,' she says, out of breath. 'The one Rosie sent to the tailor's.' She goes to hail a taxi, then turns towards Karin. 'You think she saw me?'

Karin shakes her head.

'She was much shorter than I thought,' says Helene.

They ask the taxi to stop round the corner from the shop, pay the driver and go in. It's nearly one. Just inside the glass doors people stand with tablets in their hands, swaying their hips to the music like last time. Helene asks for Rosie. An Asian girl with a ring in her nose and androgynous clothes goes off to look for her, but comes back saying that she's not there. 'She's not at work today,' she says. 'But you said Helene, right? Here you are.'

A stiff bag dangles from her fingers by pink cotton threads. Helene takes it. There's a white slip of paper stapled to the side with her name misspelled in felt pen. Helene lifts it up, as if she expects to find something else, a secret message from Rosie perhaps, but the other side is empty, apart from the ink that's bled through the paper.

'Use the fitting rooms in the men's department,' says the woman with the nose ring. 'There's usually less of a queue there. If there's anything at all you need, just say. Ask for Sonia, that's me.' She points at the black headset she has round her neck, as proof she can always be found.

They go towards the escalators. Helene stands a few steps above Karin and twiddles the threads from the bag around her index finger so the skin bulges between them. Karin senses her disappointment.

'She said she'd be here,' Helene says. 'Didn't she? Rosie, I mean. I'm sure she said that.'

'Maybe something happened.'

'Yeah.'

The difference in their heights is suddenly evened out again and Helene steps onto the shiny lino floor. A man with large gold earrings looks down the long passageway of occupied fitting rooms and gives them a red plastic disc with the number one on it. They walk past mint green curtains streaked with dust and hear rustling movements then a hollow thud, as though someone has slammed the wall to regain their balance, with their legs bundled up in tight trouser legs. They approach the mirrors on the end wall and find several empty fitting rooms up there. Karin sits down on a bench that stretches along the opposite wall. Helene reaches up to pull the curtain.

'But it's good,' Helene says, 'that Rosie has some time off, I mean. She said she wanted to see more of her son. I hope they're doing something nice.'

Karin nods. While Helene changes, she runs her fingers through her hair and imagines Rosie having breakfast at her boyfriend's with her son, the boyfriend putting his hand on her chubby thigh under the table.

After a while Helene comes out. The dress fits well, forming a soft outline of her figure. She strokes her hands uncertainly over the material. Her calves are hairless, with a web of blue veins, and she's wearing grey cotton socks with white lace edges. 'I'm going to a fortieth birthday party with Endre in a few weeks,' she says. 'I can wear it then.'

'Yes, you'll look great,' says Karin. 'It'll be great.'

Helene is thirty-three. In a few years she may have her varicose veins done so she can continue wearing skirts, as Karin and Karin's mother have done before her.

'It'll be great,' Karin says again.

Helene studies her reflection in the mirror and nods. She pulls the curtain closed behind her and Karin goes over to the wall of mirrors to check the pores around her nose. She takes some powder out of her bag. A song she remembers having heard on the radio is playing over the invisible speakers.

'I lied,' says Helene behind the curtain.

'What?'

'I lied. Something did happen last night, between me and Ed. I lied this morning.'

Karin goes closer, stroking her knuckles against the mint green fabric. It's softer than it looks. 'Can I come in?' she says. There's no answer. 'Helene, can I come in?'

'I'm nodding.'

Karin slips in behind the curtain. Helene is standing there in just her underwear, holding the dress against her chest. She's pounding her collarbone, rhythmically and vehemently, as if something will happen if she stops. The room is tiny; it's impossible to move without touching her. Karin didn't think it through before coming in. She stands completely still. 'Did you go back to his place?'

'No, outside… between some – it doesn't matter. That's not the point.' Helene sighs. 'I slept at the hotel.'

Karin doesn't know what to say. There are mirrors on three of the walls and they reflect each other many times over, all the angles visible at once.

'Now I'm just as bad,' says Helene.

'As me?' says Karin.

Helene actually smiles. 'As Endre,' she says. She looks down at her feet. 'I thought it'd feel different, but it just feels like I've got nothing.'

'What would happen if you left him?'

Helene tenses her jaw and shakes her head.

'Maybe it's actually a good thing,' says Karin after a while, 'being just as bad. It can be a starting point.'

'For what?'

'I don't know. Something more honest.'

Someone walks past the fitting room and goes into the cubicle next door. They can hear coat hangers scraping against the steel rail along the wall, heavy shoes being kicked off. Karin tentatively puts her arms round Helene. Helene doesn't speak, doesn't move, she just keeps pounding her chest, and the rhythmical movement is like a beating heart between them.

They're at the airport an hour and a half before their flight is due to leave. On a huge screen in the departures hall, a woman wades through a barren, apocalyptic landscape, lies down on her back and lets gusts of sand blow over her. It's an advert for perfume. In the duty-free shop, Helene chooses big tubes of English wine gums for the children and a deodorant twin pack for Endre, which she then puts back. 'Aluminium salts,' she explains.

Outside the plane, the tarmac is bathed in the pink light of evening. Helene sits with her cheek against the seat, looking out. She holds one hand against her stomach. Through the round window, Karin can see two young men in yellow vests and blue overalls heaving the luggage onto the conveyor belt that takes it into the cargo hold. It suddenly makes Karin think about Torstein's mother, who was tube-fed. She got a message while they were in the taxi on the way to Heathrow. *Sorry*, it said, *I just wanted to talk*. She didn't answer but did save his number again. She looks across at Helene and studies the taut tendons in her neck and the white plug in her ear. She's listening to something. Her phone is on her lap and when it lights up with a notification about the low battery, Karin sees that it's a podcast with *meditation* in the title. She tilts her head, trying to read what it says, but Helene turns to face her and removes her earbuds.

'Sorry,' says Karin. 'I was staring, I know.'

'Did you know Imke's ill?' says Helene.

Because she was expecting something else, it takes a minute for her to adjust. Karin shakes her head. It's been a long time since she's spoken to Erik, at least five or six months. The last time she saw him he had a golden whale's tooth hanging round his neck on a leather string, which he called a 'summer necklace'.

'What kind of ill?' says Karin.

'Early-onset dementia. And she's younger than you, you know, just turned fifty. It's so tragic. She only got the diagnosis a month ago. I don't even know if Dad wants me to tell you. Don't tell him I said anything.'

Karin doesn't know what to say; she just says how sad it is, that she's always liked Imke, which is partly true. Imke has a straightforward German politeness about her, and she makes it possible to have easy, superficial family get-togethers.

'Long before we knew what it was, she just behaved weirdly,' says Helene. 'Said strange things, flirted outrageously with staff in the supermarket, left Aldo in a cafe.' She pauses. 'In the summer we went for a walk in Frogner Park, just me and her, and I stopped off to buy coffee at one of those kiosks. When I came back, I saw Imke yelling at someone with a dog. I've no idea what the dog had done, probably nothing, but she went berserk. At first I was really embarrassed, ashamed, and wondered if I should turn round and leave her there. But then I noticed how everyone was looking at her as if she was insane. A group of teenagers were laughing their heads off. I got so angry. Furious.' She breathes out. 'And it felt so good.'

'Yes,' says Karin hesitantly. 'You must allow yourself to get angry.'

'That's not what I mean,' says Helene. 'You asked me what would happen if I left Endre. It's not that simple.'

The flight attendant comes past and asks Karin to lift the scarf on her lap so she can see the seat belt is properly fastened. Karin obeys; the flight attendant smiles and thanks her, then continues down the aisle, turning her head from side to side like a mechanical bird. Helene's eyes linger on Karin. Then she puts her earbuds back in again, presses the screen on her phone and looks outside. The captain introduces himself over the loudspeaker, saying they are almost ready for take-off. Then they move slowly towards the runway.

When Helene was little, they visited a flashy water park in Gran Canaria, where the biggest attraction was a killer whale. On a poster next to the aquarium, it said that the animal had been taken from the Greenland Sea right outside Iceland in the late 1970s. Underneath there was a family tree showing that the whale had had four young since it came to the park, and all of them had been bought by SeaWorld and taken to Orlando in Florida by a fleet of helicopters. The huge mammal lay floating against the window at an angle, so its back end was higher than its head, which was turned downwards towards the false seabed. For the duration of the five or six hours they spent at the park, it didn't move. Despite the unruly children who banged on the glass with sticky hands and shouted in Spanish and English and German and Danish, it lay immobile in the water.

'Is it dead?' asked Helene.

'No, I don't think so – look, it's blinking, can you see?'

They went right up to the glass and saw how the row of lashes slid back and forth over the black hemispheres like windscreen wipers. Helene crouched down and pressed a finger against the window. Then she turned back in despair. 'But why isn't it swimming? Doesn't it want to?'

'Maybe it misses its children,' said Karin without thinking.

She stands there looking at Helene and Endre's car as they drive off. The tail lights shine red against the bike shed on the bend. They didn't wait for her to go inside before they left. Helene did get out of the car to say goodbye and thank her for coming, but at the same time gave the impression that it was a formality more than anything else. When Helene opened the passenger door, Endre was staring down at his lap, probably on his phone.

On the way from the airport all three of them had mostly been silent. Endre was waiting in the arrivals hall when they came, wearing hiking trousers and a large down jacket. His skin was even and brown. He kissed Helene, hugged Karin and asked if they'd had a nice time. Then he insisted on taking both their suitcases, pulling them behind him, one in each hand. On the way to the car park, he asked what they had done together. Helene said they'd been to shops, pubs, restaurants – had a 'real girls' weekend away'. Endre said that sounded good, and opened the car from a distance with his key.

There's a cold wind blowing around her ears and a thick layer of muddy leaves on the ground under the row of planted trees. She's waiting for something, but doesn't know what. Then she unlocks the front door, carries her suitcase up all the stairs and puts it down heavily inside the door to her flat. She studies herself as usual in the mirror, registering the slight gap between expectation and reality. Even though it's late, she goes round the flat turning on the lights. The rooms are exactly how she left them. On the sitting room table there's a bunch of wilting roses; a dull film stretches upwards along the bottom of the vase and leaves lie scattered beside it. Karin puts her phone down on the table, brushes the dry leaves into her hand and goes into the kitchen to throw them in the bin. She puts away the duty-free wine bottles in the cupboard and the vodka in the freezer, but first pours some into a glass, drinks it neat, gets out the bottle and fills it up again. The chill in her throat becomes warmth in her stomach and she can relax. She looks at the clock over the oven; it's just past midnight. Tomorrow means a whole new week with no plans.

Karin lies awake in bed. The weekend replays in her head until she can bear it no longer. She goes into the kitchen, has another glass of vodka, and then another, before going back to bed. She pictures Helene in the car with Endre. She pictures them parking in the garage, sitting there for a while, silent in the dark, hearing the automatic doors creak and hum and land with a thud on the concrete. She pictures Endre turning towards Helene, taking a breath and saying he's glad to have her home again. And Helene answering that she's glad to be back, that she's missed the kids, really missed them. Then he takes her hand, and says that he's so sorry. That he never meant to hurt her. He's deeply ashamed, he says. Helene shrugs, says that's just how things are, there's nothing they can do about it now, but she lets him hold her hand on his lap for a while before she asks if they're going to go in. The engine's turned off and the car has gone cold. Endre nods, lifts her hand to his mouth and kisses it. Then he gets her suitcase out of the boot and walks behind Helene through the door from the garage. The babysitter, the girl from next door, is on her laptop in the sitting room. Endre pays her while Helene puts away the duty-free purchases in the kitchen and dims the bright light. After the babysitter has gone, Endre asks if she'd like a cup of tea before they go to bed. She shakes her head. He says that he has spent the weekend thinking, and that he's willing to make considerable changes in the future, really work on himself. He wants to start having therapy and to prioritize the family more. Helene doesn't answer. Then she says she has something for him. 'For me?' he says, surprised, and she nods, handing him a small velvet bag tied with silk thread. She says he doesn't really deserve a present, but she smiles as she says it. And when the little white stone slides out of the bag and into his palm, she tells him that it's a quartz crystal. That she has learned about crystals and this one's supposed to work as a 'soul cleanser', connecting the physical dimension with the spiritual, drawing out all types of negative energy. Endre caresses the stone pensively, holding it firmly in his fingers as he bends over to kiss her. He says he didn't know she believed in that sort of thing, in healing. She answers that she doesn't *not* believe in it, that she's willing to try to believe in things that don't immediately make sense.

They go into the bathroom together, brush their teeth and wash their faces with the same expensive face wash. While Endre flosses, Helene rubs in moisturizer. She's naked apart from her pants, and when Endre looks at her in the mirror, their eyes meet. He says she's beautiful, the most beautiful woman he knows, and she smiles, comes over and hugs him. His chest is hard and warm against her cheek; she hears his heart beating and counts the beats aloud for him. He uses mouthwash and spits it out with her arms still around him. For the first time in a long while, Helene feels that everything's going to be all right, that she can continue to love Endre and that he can love her back. It's such a huge relief that she's nearly willing to forget everything. After checking on the children in their separate rooms, caressing their warm cheeks then creeping out again, she and Endre lie in bed whispering quietly. They talk about holidays they've had, remembering in detail a house in Mallorca they rented soon after Aldo was born, during Helene's maternity leave, and which they want to rent again next summer, this time with Lea too. The whole family, says Endre. They're both lying on their sides. Endre strokes her bare arm up and down, and she becomes aware of a warm rush under her skin that's made more intense when he leans forward and kisses her. They suddenly can't wait; Helene pulls her nightie over her head and uses her feet to push down Endre's pyjama bottoms. He helps her and kicks them onto the floor. But when he pushes himself inside her, his chest against hers, she feels an almost primitive aversion. The room suddenly seems alien, and so does Endre. She breathes like a frightened animal, in a way that could easily be mistaken for pleasure. Behind his back she sees her legs. Her body adapts to anyone, she thinks, and the thought scares her. Endre moves with increasing urgency and force, whispering hot and hectic words in her ear. She feels the same panic as during take-off, that she's trapped in something that won't save her when it crashes. Her chin presses down into Endre's shoulder; she holds him firmly by his upper arms and realizes she's crying. She suddenly knows for sure that this and these feelings are real. Holding her close from behind afterwards, he whispers that he loves her, that he'll do everything he can to prove he is worthy. She lies with her knees pulled up under herself, looking down at the pants she used to wipe the semen off her stomach.

When she wakes up it's to the sound of Lea crying. She gets out of bed, ties her dressing gown round her waist and goes into the adjacent room, where Lea is standing in her cot. She lifts her and holds her against her chest with an overwhelming feeling of being home. She nestles her nose against Lea's downy head and inhales deeply, then holds up Lea's small fingers and studies them, one after the other. It's just starting to get light outside and the frost glitters on the tiles of the garage roof. The night seems long gone. She carries Lea on her hip into Aldo's room, where he's still asleep with his mouth open. After running her fingers through his fringe to wake him up gently, she remains seated on the low bed for a few minutes. She tells them about England and black taxis, about the presents that might or might not be waiting in a bag in the kitchen. While Endre showers and shaves, she helps Aldo get dressed and wash his face, finds clean clothes in the drawer and gets Lea ready for the day too. Then she has a shower herself. She closes her eyes and lets the water run over her like a catharsis while Endre makes breakfast for the children.

NEAR DISTANCE

HANNAH STOLTENBERG

First published in 2023
by Weatherglass Books

First published as *Nada* in Norway in 2019
by Gyldendal Norsk Forlag

ISBN: 978-1-7392601-7-0

Cover design: Tom Etherington
Copy-editing: Sarah Terry
Proofreading: Tessa Thornley
Typesetting: James Tookey

Printed in the U.K. by TJ Books Limited, Padstow

www.weatherglassbooks.com

This translation has been published with the financial support of NORLA

Weatherglass
Books